POPULAR HITS

OF THE

SHOWA ERA

ALSO BY RYU MURAKAMI

Audition

POPULAR HITS

OF THE

SHOWA ERA

RYU MURAKAMI

Translated by Ralph McCarthy

W. W. NORTON & COMPANY   NEW YORK · LONDON

Originally published in Japanese as *Shôwa kayô daizenshû*

For information about permission to reproduce selections from this book,
write to Permissions, W. W. Norton & Company, Inc.,
500 Fifth Avenue, New York, NY 10110

For information about special discounts for bulk purchases, please contact
W. W. Norton Special Sales at specialsales@wwnorton.com or 800-233-4830

Manufacturing by Courier Westford
Book design by Ellen Cipriano
Production manager: Devon Zahn

Library of Congress Cataloging-in-Publication Data

Murakami, Ryu, 1952–
[Showa kayo daizenshu. English]
Popular hits of the Showa era / Ryu Murakami ;
translated by Ralph McCarthy.
p. cm.
"Originally published in Japanese as Shôwa kayô daizenshû"
ISBN 978-0-393-33842-3 (pbk.)
I. Title.
PL856.U696S4913 2011
895.6'35—dc22

2010031109

W. W. Norton & Company, Inc.
500 Fifth Avenue, New York, N.Y. 10110
www.wwnorton.com

W. W. Norton & Company Ltd.
Castle House, 75/76 Wells Street, London W1T 3QT

1 2 3 4 5 6 7 8 9 0

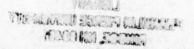

POPULAR HITS
OF THE
SHOWA ERA

1

Season of Love

Ishihara had had a feeling, ever since the party the night before, that something like this was going to happen. That he alone had had this feeling was decidedly not because he was more intelligent than the others, or more skillful at analyzing situations, or psychic or anything. Ishihara had a tendency to burst into mindless and uncontrollable laughter at random moments, and it was a tendency he shared with all the other members of the group. The only difference was that in the interval between one bout of laughter and the next, into his head alone some sort of image—if not an actual idea—would occasionally pop.

The party had begun as usual at seven in the evening, and more or less everyone had been there—Ishihara, Nobue, Yano, Sugiyama, Kato, and Sugioka. "More or less" because no one was keeping track, but in fact the six of them constituted everyone. They assembled as always at Nobue's apartment in Chofu City, on the western edge of Greater Tokyo. Each of them brought food or drinks in a plastic bag or paper sack or, in one case, an old-school *furoshiki* wrapping cloth. Yano was the one with the furoshiki. He also wore his prized Leica M6 on a strap around his neck.

"Check it out, I saw Karinaka Rie—the adult video actress?—at this street fair in Shinjuku the other day, and I took a bunch of pictures of her, but would you believe it? None of 'em turned out. I don't know why. I mean, I don't get it. Why would that happen? I've thought about it and thought about it, but . . ."

Stroking the Leica with his right index finger, Yano expanded upon this mystery at some length, but, typically enough, none of the others responded or reacted in any way. These gatherings didn't have the atmosphere one normally associates with the word "party." Nobue's apartment, just north of Chofu Station, was in an old two-story wood-frame-and-stucco building with a sizable parking lot in the rear. The six members of the group generally assembled here of a Saturday evening, but the gatherings had no clear purpose, and one hesitates even to call the participants "friends," since they lacked any common goals or interests. Nobue and Ishihara had been classmates in high school; Yano had met Ishihara in the computer section of a bookstore, where they'd exchanged remarks about the new Macintosh being this or that and then, having nothing better to do, meandered off to a coffee shop and sat facing each other for a couple of hours, neither of them talking much but each coming to the general conclusion that the other was a person rather like himself, the upshot of which was that they'd swapped phone numbers and become comrades of sorts; Sugiyama, the only one over thirty, had met Yano while temping at a construction site out near Chiba; Kato was a sort of underling or sidekick of Sugiyama's; and Sugioka knew Nobue somehow or other.

Nobue was the one who'd originally suggested a party. It had now been about a year since the first time they'd assembled at his apartment. No preparations of any sort had been made for that first gathering, and no one brought anything to eat or drink. They'd all been to parties before, of course, but it had never occurred to any of them to think about how to host one or prepare for one, much less be the life of one. There were only five of them at the first party—Nobue, Ishihara, Yano, Sugiyama, and Kato. Kato, having lost a brief rock-paper-scissors showdown, was sent out to the vending machine down the street to purchase a sackful of One Cup Sake drinks, and when he returned they all sat around quietly sipping from the little glass containers. Every now and then one of them would burst into mindless laughter or relate in a fragmented way some personal anecdote, fully cognizant of the fact that no one else was listening, and after some five hours of this the party just sort of evaporated.

Not until the fourth time they gathered had the parties begun to take shape. There was a full moon that night. Sugiyama had brought an armful of karaoke laser discs, and though no one in the group could sing, a few of them hummed along tentatively. They were humming to one of the tracks when a light went on in the window of an apartment across the parking lot, and there, clearly visible from where they sat, a young woman with very long legs and an unbelievable body was in the act of disrobing. Sipping at their sake in awed silence, all six of them watched, along with the full moon, as this modest striptease unfolded. The young woman with the unbelievable body was immediately elevated to the status of everyone's special idol, and the karaoke set (which had apparently conjured her up) to that of a miracle machine more worthy of reverence than even their precious computers. Karaoke became an essential element of each party from that night on, and they all began memorizing lyrics and timidly attempting to sing. Months went by, however, without the young woman with the unbelievable body making a return appearance. It was at the sixth party, when she'd failed to materialize for the second consecutive time, that Nobue proposed the post-party ritual that was to become such an important part of their lives. For someone in this group to come up with and propose an idea, and for the others to actually listen to it, consider it, voice their opinions, come to a consensus, and act upon it, was an unprecedented event—an event of historical significance to rival the moment seven or eight million years ago when some ancestor of human beings first stood upright and blundered forward on two feet.

The evolution of the parties had been slow but inexorable. At the third party, Ishihara had arrived bearing *eihire* (dried stingray fin), *kusamochi* (mugwort rice cakes), and *piisen* (peanuts mixed with tiny rice crackers), and from then on everyone began bringing things to eat or drink. At the ninth party a small wave of panic had swept the room when Sugioka showed up not with the usual dry snacks like stingray fin or peanuts or chocolate but a packaged macaroni salad of the sort sold in delicatessens and supermarkets. Nobue took one look at the macaroni salad and, after the inevitable bout of spasmodic laughter, set out plates and forks for all. One could have searched each individual brain cell in Nobue's head—and everyone else's, for that matter—without finding so much as a hint that the concept of providing others with eating utensils would ever occur, but it had, and it was a deeply moving moment. Sugioka, who'd bought the macaroni salad at a butcher's shop just down the road, near his own apartment, actually misted up on seeing his purchase cause such excitement and wield such unexpected influence. At the tenth party, it was Yano's turn to stir the others to their depths by bringing six portions of Nagasaki Chanmen, an instant noodle dish that required only the addition of boiling water. Such astonishing mutations in the nature of the parties were, Nobue and Ishihara and the others all believed, directly attributable to karaoke; and the scale of the all-important post-party ritual continued to expand.

It was during the party on the second Saturday of June, the sort of muggy rainy-season evening when air, underclothes, and feelings all reach saturation point, that Ishihara became aware of the unwonted anxiety taking shape inside him.

Unfamiliarity with anxiety was something all members of this group had in common. In other ways, however, they couldn't have been less alike. All but a couple of them were from different parts of the country, and their social backgrounds and economic circumstances varied considerably. Complicating matters further was the fact that you couldn't have judged who was what simply by looking at them. Whereas Nobue, for example, looked as if he might be a scion of old money, he was in fact the third son of a day laborer in the *mikan* orchards of Shizuoka; whereas Yano, when viewed in a certain light and from a certain angle, might have passed for someone who'd graduated from an elite university, he had in fact once been addicted to the toxic and long-unfashionable toluene, the fumes of which he had inhaled on a daily basis with high school friends, all of whom came down with debilitating nerve disorders as a result, while Yano himself, hardy though slight, maintained his health but was caught huffing the stuff on one of his rare visits to school and summarily expelled, which meant that he was officially a middle school graduate; and whereas Sugiyama, for example, to judge from his lugubrious face and sickly complexion, might have been on the verge of slitting his own wrists, he in fact tended to burst into laughter even more frequently and unexpectedly than the others, to the extent that even they sometimes looked at him askance. These young men, in other words, represented a variety of types, but one thing they had in common was that they'd all given up on committing positively to anything in life. This was not their fault, however. The blame lay with a certain ubiquitous spirit of the times, transmitted to them by their respective mothers. And perhaps it goes without saying that this "spirit of the times" was in fact an oppressive value system based primarily upon the absolute certainty that nothing in this world was ever going to change.

If these six young men had anything else in common it was

something rather difficult to explain, except perhaps as a certain kind of strength on what we might call the cellular level. And this strength is what gave all of them, even in the absence of any good jokes or clever puns or amusing incidents, the ability to laugh to a more or less abnormal degree.

It wasn't as if they would laugh together, mind you. They laughed individually, at completely different moments, and not necessarily about anything in particular. Each laughed in his own distinctive way, but in each case the laughter was loud, uncontrollable, and spasmodic, like sneezes or hiccups. An impartial observer would have noticed that at any given moment at least one of the six would be laughing—that by the time the laughter of one had subsided, that of another would have begun, which is in effect to say that the laughs never ceased—but the same observer would not have had the impression that anyone was actually having fun. Perhaps for these young men, all born in the latter half of the Showa Era, the connection between fun and laughter had simply never been made.

Such, then, was the atmosphere of the party at which Ishihara began to experience his anxious foreboding. The night wore on as always. A few members of the group recounted incidents from their own lives while nobody listened and a continuous, idiotic cackling echoed off the walls; but even when it was time to begin practicing their rock-paper-scissors technique, Ishihara's anxiety lingered. The track to the theme song for tonight's ritual, Pinky & the Killers' "Season of Love," played softly over the speakers, and everyone started trying to approximate the main vocal, each imagining himself in the role of the lovely and charming Pinky.

Ishihara was startled by how tangible the anxiety was inside him. He'd never experienced anything like this before. He was certain it wasn't simply a matter of his having suddenly uncovered a dread that had always been there. No, this was definitely something new. It was shaped like a fetus. And just as a fetus in the later stages of pregnancy kicks the walls of the womb to assert its own existence, the anxiety fetus was sending Ishihara an eerie, wavelike signal that seemed to say, *Don't even think about forgetting I'm here!* The signal disrupted and weakened his heartbeat intermittently and caused the image of a tiny, undeveloped human being, its back curled forward and a cord extending from its navel like an unspooling fire hose, to blink on and off in his mind. He tried again and again to distract himself by laughing idiotically. His laughter was so droolingly mindless, in fact, and so explosive, that the others began to wonder if he hadn't lost his wits, and Nobue whispered to Yano, "If he gets any weirder, we'll take him somewhere and dump him, okay?"

Yano, who had long harbored an ambition to abandon something, experienced a little thrill at these words and unconsciously tightened his grip on the Leica M6. He had purchased the Leica from a man with a glass eye at a little camera shop in Hong Kong, where he'd gone on an employee excursion organized by the company he worked for and advertised as a *gurumei tsuaa* ("gourmet tour"), which to his surprise turned out to mean that they were to wander around as a group, eating at different restaurants. The Leica wasn't his first camera, of course—for years he had carried an Olympus Pen given him by his father—but only recently had it dawned on him that the reason he was devoted to photography wasn't because he particularly enjoyed capturing an image in a frame but because pointing the lens at an object and snapping the shutter was a way of virtually abandoning that object. Photography therefore provided a certain degree of catharsis for Yano, but he would have preferred to abandon an actual "thing"—or, if at all possible, an actual "person."

A strange old tale had recently been revived in popular novels and films about a man who in accordance with the rules of the social group in which he lives must leave his aged mother to die on a desolate mountaintop. It was a story that would surely have caused any self-respecting immigrant or refugee or descendant of slaves to gag in disgust, but it was the stuff of Yano's deepest aspirations. If only he could be given a chance to abandon something of tremendous importance to him—to dump it as if it were no longer needed in his life! He often reflected that if he were a woman, all he'd have to do was get pregnant, give birth to the baby, and abandon it; and it had even occurred to him that if he dressed up in drag and left a Cabbage Patch Kid somewhere he might be able to experience a similar sort of sensation, though he was restrained by the fear that if he went that far he might never find his way back. *I am, after all, a man, for better or worse,* he would mutter, and resign himself once again to waiting for a gender-appropriate opportunity to appear.

Ishihara, after fraying everyone's nerves with his astonishing cachinnations, finally settled down and began practicing rock-paper-scissors, as the others were already doing. The rock-

paper-scissors contest was what one might call the prelude to
the all-important ritual, and though it goes without saying that
rock-paper-scissors isn't the sort of thing you can actually practice, each in his own particular way was convinced that he was
doing exactly that. Nobue, for example, was loudly blustering
that "Yano always starts out with rock, right? And with Sugiyama
it's always paper, right?"—though of course no one was listening.
Yano stared at his own hand, studying the shape of each rock,
paper, and scissors he formed. He was particularly concerned
with his scissors and kept adjusting the angle between the index
and middle fingers, muttering to himself as he did so: "When two
lines of the same length describe an angle of elevation, the trigo-
nometric function of the corresponding isosceles triangle must
differ depending upon whether you're talking Euclidean or non-
Euclidean, so, um . . ." Sugioka was pitting his right hand against
his left and plaintively asking, "Which do you think is the real
me?"—but needless to say no one paid any attention. Kato was
trying to read his own left palm, believing as he did in the theory
that vibrations produced by one's opponent's mood could cause
a delicate alteration in the pattern of lines there: "If the lifeline
twitches—even a tiny bit—it means the enemy's coming with
paper, see?" Sugiyama was rubbing his right palm with a chunk
of ice. "After all," he mumbled, "even your balls get tougher if you
ice 'em." Ishihara held his right hand on top of his head and was
making rocks and scissors and announcing, "Rock!" or "Scissors!" as he did so. "How come I always know which one I'm
going to choose," he wondered aloud, "and no one else does?"

  Tonight, in addition to One Cup Sake, they were drinking
beer and wine. As for cuisine, beef jerky took the starring role.

There was also macaroni salad—that begetter of a new era—not to mention various dry snacks, but none of these could compete with the headliner in terms of aroma and sheer visual appeal. The beef jerky had been supplied by Kato, who worked for a small importer of foodstuffs. Kato subsisted almost entirely on his company's products, but it had never before occurred to him that the things he ate every day could lend pomp to a party. His main staple was giant corn from Peru, though when he wanted meat he would grab a package of this same beef jerky—produced by the American firm Tengu—and rehydrate the strips by boiling them in water à la sukiyaki. When he sensed that his body needed veggies he would open a can of apricots preserved in syrup—a product of the People's Republic of China—never for a moment doubting that the apricot was a vegetable. He'd brought the beef jerky on this particular evening thinking only that it might mildly please the others, but in fact it was a sensation. When he casually plopped the four packages of Tengu teriyaki-style down on the tatami mats of Nobue's apartment, a rare hush fell over the room. It wasn't that none of them had ever eaten beef jerky before. But the excess energy that they themselves knew least what to do with helped lend an otherworldly glow to this austere food product, so redolent of the frontier spirit. None of them said a word, but with an intensity that might have made an impartial observer wonder how they would react to something like stone crab, they began tearing the jerky to shreds and wolfing it down.

Complemented with wine from Yamanashi and Portugal, the beef jerky had rapidly disappeared; Ishihara had ceased laughing like an idiot; and preparations for the rock-paper-scissors show-down were in full swing. But just as they were about to start the actual competition, Nobue made a discovery that turned their entire world upside down.

It seemed an eternity since they'd last seen a light in the window of the room across the parking lot. That light was on now, and through the lace curtains they could make out the silhouette of the woman with the unbelievable body. Sugiyama instantly grew so tense that he squeaked and probably would have gibbered had he not bitten his own left hand. The woman with the unbelievable body was brushing her long hair, and now she casually tossed it back over her shoulders with two or three graceful flicks of her fingers. That was enough to elicit a commotion of sighs and exclamations from Nobue and the others, and Ishihara went so far as to mutter, "Anyone mind if I jerk off?" He wasn't the only one who was thinking of masturbation, but even as the woman undid the buttons on her blouse, the sublime aura of inviolability she radiated through the curtains prevented them from putting any such thoughts into action. The blouse slid off, the lines of her shoulders and back were revealed, and as she began to wriggle out of her skirt, tears welled up in Yano's and Sugioka's and Kato's eyes. "This must be what it's like to see a UFO, or the earth from the space shuttle," Nobue murmured, and everyone nodded breathlessly. The woman shrugged out of her slip and unhooked her brassiere, and then her silhouette disappeared from view.

"Shower time!" shouted Ishihara, and the other five responded almost in unison, like the chorus in a grade-school play:

That's right! That's right! It's shower time!

"She's going to take a shower now!"

A shower now!

"A nice, hot, steamy, sexy shower now!"

Shower now!

"The shower is a miracle!"

A miracle! A miracle!

"From all those, like, little pinholes in that weird-shaped thing . . ."

Weird-shaped thing . . .

"Hot water shoots out—just think of it!"

Just think of it!

"It's got to be a miracle!"

It is! It is a miracle!

It was only by vigorously chanting this odd sort of call-and-response that the six of them managed to master the excitement bubbling up from deep inside. They now breathed a collective sigh and sat back to finish off the wine and beer, basking in the afterglow of perfect happiness.

And then, at last, the rock-paper-scissors contest began.

The theme song for the evening's ritual, as has been noted, was "Season of Love." Instead of the usual "*Jan–ken–pon*," therefore, you had to count off saying, "Jan–ken–PINKY!"

Nobue was the first to be eliminated, and he collapsed on the tatami mats and thrashed about in despair and frustration. According to the rules, he must now serve as the driver for the night. Sugiyama tossed him the keys, and he slunk outside to warm up the HiAce's engine.

The ultimate victory went to Ishihara. On conquering his final opponent, he leapt into the air, shouting, "I did it!"—and the moment he uttered these words, the anxiety returned in the form of a chilling question: *Is it really all right to be this happy?*

As it turned out, of course, Ishihara's anxiety knew exactly what it was talking about.

Because this evening's song was to be "Season of Love," it was necessary to determine only first place (lead singer), last place (driver), and fifth place (engineer/roadie). Naturally, if the theme song had been something by Uchiyamada Hiroshi & Cool Five or Danny Iida & Paradise King or the Three Funkys or Three Graces, it would have called for a different ranking system altogether.

Ishihara was so thrilled to have garnered first place that he squealed and began to perform the dance the others called "The Ishihara." The incomprehensible anxiety was still at work, but it had occurred to him that if he moved his body maybe everything would work itself out. There is a rodent known as the tremuggia that makes its home in the Kalahari Desert and looks like a cross between a chipmunk and a rat, and though there's no reason to believe that Ishihara was aware of the fact, this dance of his closely resembled that creature's mating ritual. He bent his knees slightly, stuck out his hindquarters, held his wrists limply at chest level, and bobbed up and down while emitting a distinctive cry: *Kuun! Kuun! Kuun!*

They all carried their things to the HiAce step van and climbed aboard. Yano, who had been the second to be eliminated, took an inventory of the equipment, and when he gave the thumbs-up, Nobue steered the HiAce out to the street and accelerated. In tense anticipation of the ritual, all of the passengers were muttering to themselves—mostly about the brief striptease they'd just watched the woman with the unbelievable body perform. In the dark rear of the van, Sugiyama had narrowed his already narrow eyes until they seemed to form a single line behind his glasses. "That was amazing, amazing," he mumbled. "Amazing, it was." Kato was tenderly touching the spot on the back of his head where the hair was thinning. "Well, that was a shocker," he muttered, "but the real test still lies ahead." It's doubtful if even he knew what that was supposed to mean.

Piloted by Nobue, the HiAce crossed the Tama River, sped past Yomiuri Land, entered the Tomei Expressway at the Kawasaki Interchange, and veered down the Odawara-Atsugi Road to Ninomiya, where it exited via the Seisho Bypass and finally rolled to a stop at a deserted spot by the coast that Yano and Kato had discovered. Last-place Nobue was sent to appraise the location by staking out a spot on the beach for a full twenty minutes, as stipulated by the guidelines. He had to make sure the place really was deserted. Once, a vacant lot Yano had found on a warehouse-lined street along Tokyo Bay turned out to be the occasional site of some sort of illicit transactions, and they'd been attacked by a pair of youths on motorcycles who smashed the windows of their van. Nobue and Ishihara and the others all hated that sort of thing. It wasn't violence that they disliked, mind you. Sugiyama had been studying karate and kick-boxing since middle school and had a habit of going off on opponents who were clearly capable of pounding him into the ground, as a result of which he'd had his skull fractured on four separate occasions; Yano had inadvertently joined a fascist youth organization when he was eighteen and as part of his training had hunted field mice with a crossbow in the remote mountains of Nagano; Nobue and Ishihara had both scored a number of knockouts in drunken brawls—although, admittedly, only when given the chance to attack unsuspecting opponents from behind; Sugioka, who owned a collection of more than a hundred edged weapons ranging from box cutters to Japanese swords, always carried one or two blades and was forever stabbing walls and tree trunks and leather sacks stuffed with sawdust, and when especially piqued had even been known to slash to ribbons the shiny skin of used blow-up dolls; and Kato suffered a chronic, obsessive delusion that sooner or later he would murder—slowly and methodically—an infant or toddler or some other weak and defenseless being, and had come recently to believe that the only way to rid himself of this obsession was to go ahead and act it out. No, it wasn't violence they disliked: it was contact with strangers. What these young men feared and hated more than anything else was being spoken to by people they hadn't met, or having to explain themselves to people they didn't know.

"It's just like Kato said, not a soul around. A stray dog wandered by with a fish head in his mouth, but I threw a rock at him. Aimed right at his balls, but I missed, but he ran away anyway."

The other five greeted Nobue's announcement with a cheer that sounded more like a collective moan, then grabbed their things and piled out of the van. Nobue and Yano, peons for the night, had to carry all the heavy equipment: spools of thick extension cord, the 3CCD Hi8 video camera and tripod, the five-hundred-watt pinspots and their stands, a gargantuan boombox, Bose speakers, and a set of Sennheiser microphones. They huffed and wheezed as they lugged everything down the narrow concrete steps to the beach, while Ishihara and the others changed into their costumes: flared velvet pantaloons, patent-leather shoes, frilled silk shirts, cummerbunds, bow ties, and tuxedo jackets with velvet lapels, followed by the top hats, false mustaches, black canes, and white gloves—for the others, that is. Ishihara alone applied bright red lipstick, false eyelashes, and a Cleopatra-style wig, tittering maniacally as he did so: *Hee hee hee hee hee hee hee hee!* Finally, decked out exactly as Pinky & the Killers had been back in the day, the performers strode down to the beach and stood there facing the sea and the tiny lights of fishing boats far offshore. Ishihara stepped forward and raised his little finger as he took the mike and cooed, "Ready, baby." Yano, off to one side, turned on the pinspots, and the intro to "Season of Love" came blasting out of the Bose 501 speaker system and echoing across the dark sea and sky. When the first line of the lyric—*I just can't seem to forget*—reverberated toward the waves in Ishihara's nausea-inducing voice, all the crabs on the beach scuttled simultaneously into their holes. As for Ishihara himself, he actually *was* able to forget—at least during the time he was singing—the anxiety growing inside him.

The day after the ritual, that anxiety revealed what it was made of.

The catalyst for it all was a badly hungover Sugioka. After backing up Ishihara on "Season of Love" more than forty times and walking the short distance home from Nobue's apartment, Sugioka remained too pumped up to sleep, so he chewed some oval sleeping tablets he'd bought from a pasty-faced girl while loafing about in Shibuya one day and washed them down with beer. This knocked him out at last, but he woke at ten in the morning feeling as if his body were made of a particularly dense type of cement. He was irritable and grumpy, as anyone might be under such circumstances, and every part of him seemed in suspended animation except for the squirmy, itchy nerve that connected his lower parts—that is to say, his penis—directly to the corresponding section of his brain. Sugioka had experienced this sensation any number of times, but today it was incomparably worse than ever before, and he spent several long minutes wondering whether to watch an adult video and masturbate until the head of his organ was raw, or to pay a visit to the Pink Salon just outside the south exit of Chofu Station, or to seek satisfaction with Eriko, a blow-up doll to whom he still hadn't put the knife and who boasted, according to her brochure, Super-Tight Anal Sensation; until weighing the pros and cons of each alternative became such a great bleeding pain in and of itself that he sliced up a perfectly good buckwheat-husk pillow with the twenty-centimeter blade of his Swedish mountain commando knife and stalked out onto the streets of Chofu, squinting in the daylight. Having secured the knife between his belt and jeans, beneath his vinyl raincoat, he was walking along the narrow road behind the Ito Yokado superstore when he noticed a stocky woman in her late thirties—a typical, not to say stereotypical, "Auntie" or Oba-san—apparently on her way home from shopping. The Oba-san was wearing a gauzy vintage white dress and dangling plastic grocery bags stuffed with clams and egg tofu and celery and curry rolls and what have you. Sweat beaded her forehead and dampened her underarms, exuding a strange mixture of odors, and she walked with her ass sticking out. To

Sugioka's bloodshot eyes, it looked as if that ass were saying, *DO ME*—or rather, the Japanese equivalent, *SHI-TE*. And in fact the wrinkles in the back of her dress seemed to spell out the word in hiragana:

して

So ya want me to do ya, do ya? thought Sugioka, and quickened his pace until he was just behind the Oba-san and able to get a closer view. From the immediate rear, she was the most ludicrous-looking creature he'd ever seen. Up until then the most ludicrous-looking had been a hippopotamus that was emptying its bladder, a sight that had emblazoned itself on his memory during a childhood field trip to the zoo, but the Oba-san's calves bulged with red and blue veins and bristled with a number of stubbly black hairs. *Hideous*, thought Sugioka. When he was within perhaps fifty centimeters his nose detected the clams and he spotted several long, wiry hairs growing from a big black mole on the back of the Oba-san's neck. *The poor thing!* he thought, and tears welled up in his eyes. He was still shuffling along half a step behind her when they came alongside a grade school athletic ground where several little boys were playing soccer, and just as a tall kid with the number 6 on his jersey scored a goal with a diving header, Sugioka gave a thrust of his hips to poke the Oba-san's ass with his foremost appendage.

The look on her face as she spun around.

Perspiration was melting her makeup, outrage dilated her nostrils, her badly penciled-on eyebrows twitched indignantly, and she appeared to be on the verge of spewing green foam. Sugioka didn't realize he was grinning; all he knew was that he had a hard-on like a tree. He thrust his hips forward a few more times, and the Oba-san began wailing like a fire-engine. "Aaaooooooooooh! Pervert! Aaoooooooooooooh! What do you think you're doing? I'll call for help!" Sugioka, disrespected by what seemed to him the lowest form of life on earth, now caught a powerful whiff of ripening clams wafting up from the Oba-san's lower regions. Seized with a nameless fear, he pulled out his commando knife, pressed the blade against the still-wailing siren of her throat, and sliced horizontally. Her neck opened as if it were a second mouth, and there was a whooshing sound followed immediately by a gusher of blood. Sugioka snickered to himself as he ran away. He glanced back just in time to see the Oba-san crumple to the pavement.

There was no one else on the street.

2

Stardust Trails

The murdered woman's name was Yanagimoto Midori, and the first one to discover the body—or, rather, the first to do anything about it—was a friend of hers named Henmi Midori. After Sugioka's hurried departure from the scene, a total of eleven people had passed the spot where Yanagimoto Midori lay with bubbles of blood burbling from her throat, but they all pretended not to see her—although it would have been impossible to miss her on a street like this, barely wide enough for two cars to scrape past. Her frilly white dress was saturated with red; the curry-filled

buns she'd bought lay squashed beside her, the yellow curry
smeared over the concrete like vomit; and in the torrid sunlight
breaking through the rainy-season clouds, the clams that had
spilled and scattered from her shopping bag promptly began to
broadcast the fragrance of decaying shellfish. Each of the eleven
passersby caught at least a glimpse of Yanagimoto Midori before
looking away and pretending they hadn't. A young housewife,
walking by with a toddler who pointed and said, "Look, Mama!
That lady's lying on the ground!" went so far as to scold her
child: "Don't look! The lady's just playing!" When a passing prep
school student saw the victim, his first instinct was to try and
help her, or at least summon the police, but he was wearing a
white shirt and on his way to a date. "Sorry, Oba-san," he muttered as he walked on. "I can't mess up this shirt. Besides," he
reasoned to himself, "there's a big pile of shit or something right
next to her."

Yanagimoto Midori's heart had stopped beating a mere fifty
seconds after Sugioka slit her throat, so it wasn't as if trying to
help her sit up or notifying the police might have saved her,
but any undue delay in acknowledging the discovery of one's
remains is of course a serious blow to one's pride. By the time
Henmi Midori came upon her dead friend and screamed her
nickname—"*Nagiiiii!*"—the latter was scarcely recognizable.
In her agony, Yanagimoto Midori had clawed at her wound and
her face. Part of her esophagus now protruded from the gash in
her throat, along with various blood vessels; a good ten centimeters of tongue sagged from one side of her mouth; her right
eyeball had been gouged from the parent socket; and her right
fist gripped a clump of hair she'd torn from her own head. Bending down for a closer look, Henmi Midori accidentally added

to the mess by vomiting explosively upon her friend's ravaged face, and it was just after doing so that she spotted a vital piece of evidence. It was a little silvery badge that had fallen from Sugioka's raincoat as he'd turned to flee the scene. Before the police arrived, Henmi Midori instinctively plucked the badge from the ground and dropped it into her handbag.

Yanagimoto Midori had been divorced and living alone, her ex having assumed custody of their only son, so her group of friends, known collectively as the Midori Society, took it upon themselves to host the wake. Shortly after ten p.m. the last of the relatives and acquaintances left, followed by the ex-husband and child, but the Midoris remained. All of them—Henmi Midori, Iwata Midori, Takeuchi Midori, Suzuki Midori, and Tomiyama Midori—shared with the late Yanagimoto the same given name. They had met one another in hobby circles and culture centers and what have you, and though their backgrounds differed considerably, they had in common the fact that each was alone and inept at making friends. They had now been associating for several years, however, all on the basis of, "My! Your name is Midori too?" Tonight, with the remains of Yanagimoto Midori before them, they all wept profusely. From time to time one of them stifled her sobs to say, "And she was such a good person!" or "To think we'll never hear Nagii sing 'Stardust Trails' again!" or "Was it just me, or did her ex-husband look sort of relieved?"—but as usual none of them seemed to hear anything the others had to say. These women were all unmistakably of the fearsome tribe known as Oba-san. Born in the middle of the Showa Era, they were all in their late thirties, all originally from somewhere outside Tokyo, all graduates of high school or junior college, all sturdy of frame and far from beautiful, all karaoke enthusiasts, and all strangers to Orgasmus. The late Yanagimoto Midori was not the only one in the group who hadn't managed to sustain a successful marriage. They were all divorcees, some with children and some without. Tomiyama Midori had been through three husbands and shared a son with ex number two, and Takeuchi Midori had given birth at seventeen to a daughter who'd grown up to marry a foreigner and now lived in Canada.

As they wept, all five were overwhelmed with a feeling they'd never experienced before. Having come face-to-face with the sobering fact that we all must die eventually, had nothing to do with it. And it wasn't that they shared the sorrow Yanagimoto Midori must have felt as she lay dying so outrageously and unexpectedly, her body and clothing fouled with her own blood and gore. Nor was it the sadness of losing a friend with whom they had all shared, if not an actual intimacy, at least the custom of getting together occasionally and chattering away without the inconvenience of having to listen to one another. No, the unfamiliar feeling the five remaining Midoris were experiencing was the sense that someone had made fools of them.

It wasn't as if the Midoris had lacked men in their lives. Though none of them had managed to achieve lasting relationships, neither had they ever experienced anything they recognized as loneliness. Each was the type of woman who refuses to depend on anyone else. Having made their way through life without ever providing or receiving comfort and affection, none of them had acquired many friends, and they had advanced well into their thirties before finding each other and forming this group of like-minded individuals. They would get together to chat, or to eat brunch at a hotel buffet, or to sing karaoke, or to swim and sunbathe at a public pool, but they never delved into one another's personal lives. When one of them said something—if, for example, Henmi Midori were to say, "Listen to this, yesterday this guy at my office who has a reputation for being quite the sex fiend? As we were leaving work it was raining and he'd forgotten his umbrella and was getting all wet so I let him in under mine, and as we're walking along he suddenly looks at me and goes, 'Henmi-san, would you like to FUCK?' Can you imagine? I just glared at him like, *How dare you!* And then he tells me that six of the eight women he's said something like that to have gone for it, that the direct approach makes them wet. I'm like, *Women aren't wet all the time, buster!* But he doesn't get it. I mean, he's incapable of recognizing anyone else's point of view, you know what I mean?"—none of the others would pay any attention to what she was actually saying, but one of them might happen to hear and latch on to some particular detail, such as the word "umbrella," and begin relating an essentially unrelated experience of her own: "I know, I know, that sort of thing happens all the time, doesn't it? Once I didn't have an umbrella, and this man named Sakakibara in my office who's forty and still single but not necessarily a homo but if you ask me it's hard to know what he's up to, he was standing in front of me and it was pouring and I was thinking he was going to let me in under his umbrella but instead he goes to practice his golf swing with it and almost hits me in the face! But I mean it's typical. Things like that happen all the time nowadays. There's so many weirdos out there!"

Nonetheless, for reasons that weren't entirely clear to anyone, the Midori Society had remained intact for a little over four years now. No one—not even the Midoris themselves—could have said what the determining factor was in creating their particular type of personality, but they all had an instinctive distaste for any action that smacked of "healing one's wounds." In fact, the responsibility for this lay with their fathers, but none of the ladies were aware of this or cared about such things, and in any case their male parents have nothing to do with our story. To open up to another person and talk about the sources of one's current anxieties, to have that person accept it all as "normal," and thereby to heal, was the sort of thing all the Midoris found despicable. For whatever reason, they couldn't afford to be conscious of their wounds. The strange, unfamiliar feeling they experienced as they sat weeping before the corpse of Yanagimoto Midori, therefore, was nothing less than an implacable rage brought on by the realization that the "wound" had come from the outside world to open them up by the throat.

They continued to weep for more than three hours after everyone else had left. Tomiyama Midori, the first to stop sobbing, began in a tiny voice to sing "Stardust Trails," a perfect match for the rhythm of the rain against the reinforced concrete wall of their late friend's one-bedroom apartment; and one by one, as they stopped weeping, the others joined in. It was the first time in the four years of their association that all of them had sung the same song together. They sang it again and again, reprising "Stardust Trails" for more than an hour, and it was only when they were done singing that Henmi Midori produced the silver badge and held it up for all to see.

"I found this at the scene of the crime," she said. "Does anyone know what it is?" The badge was passed around from hand to hand. "I believe it belonged to the murderer."

Suzuki Midori said, "I saw where that stupid-looking detective was saying it seemed to be a random killing, which meant they might never find the murderer," and Iwata Midori said, "I read in the local news section that the police are looking for eyewitnesses," and Tomiyama Midori said, "I know this badge!

"I see my son once a week, right? So I always want to feed him something delicious, because his father's a man with no ambition whatsoever and I'm afraid he's robbed the poor boy of even the will to eat delicious things, which it would be better if he lived with me but I have to work and I know my son understands that, but anyway he always wants to eat at MOS Burger, teriyaki burgers with double mayonnaise, three of them, and then we go to this store called Kiddy Kastle, and out in front of the store is a video game he likes to play, and if you score over three hundred thousand points you get one of these badges, and there's a poster with a list of all the people who've won a badge."

For the very first time, only one person was talking, and everyone else in the group was listening.

"So if we investigate all the names on the list, I bet we'll find the killer."

Tomiyama Midori stopped there, and an eerie silence filled the room. It was a silence pregnant with heart-tingling anticipation, the sort of thing the Midori Society experienced only rarely—most recently when the six of them had decided to take their first trip abroad together (and ended up on a five-day,

four-night excursion to Singapore and Hong Kong). None of the
Midoris had ever been big on travel, and though they were always
trying to think of things to do together, somehow the idea of
going overseas had never before occurred to them. Every one of
them had always thought of travel abroad as an extravagance she
had no need for. They believed it was wrong to want things you
didn't need, and that the people who flaunted Celine scarves,
for example, or Louis Vuitton bags or Chanel belts or Hermès
perfumes, were essentially people who had no self-esteem.
Somewhere deep in their internal organs the Midoris carried the
conviction that buying such things was just an attempt, albeit on
an extremely primitive level, to "heal one's wounds," but it goes
without saying that they too aspired to Celine and Louis Vuitton
and Chanel and Hermès, not to mention world travel. Which
was why, on that day when they'd gathered at Suzuki Midori's
apartment for a dubious culinary experience billed as "Box
Lunches of Seven Major Train Stations" and Iwata Midori said,
"How about taking a trip overseas, somewhere nearby maybe?"
this same sort of tingly silence had descended. Everyone was
thrilled but hesitated to be the first to admit it.

"So we find out who the killer is . . . and then what?" Henmi
Midori, who tended to overdo the facial packs and whose forehead and cheeks shone so brightly as a result that they reflected
the individual bulbs in the ceiling lamp, spoke these words, and
there followed another, even deeper silence. All five lowered their
eyes shyly, like young ladies meeting a proposed marriage partner for the first time and finding him just to their liking. Iwata
Midori plucked at the loose threads of the carpet next to her
cushion; Henmi Midori unclenched an incipient fist and gazed
at her fingernails; Takeuchi Midori hummed tunelessly; Suzuki

Midori raised her empty beer glass to her lips; and Tomiyama Midori fluttered her long false eyelashes—the kind you don't often see anymore.

No one spoke, so Henmi Midori, discoverer of Yanagimoto Midori's corpse, took her question a step further.

"Are we going to kill him ourselves?"

What followed was the deepest silence yet.

On Saturday of that week, Tomiyama Midori met her son, Osamu, at a station on the Keio Line. "How's your father?" she asked, stroking his hair and reflecting that she couldn't care less how his father was, and as always Osamu just tilted his head to one side and didn't reply. Tomiyama Midori loved this unaffable child of hers, however, as only a mother could. In fact, it was only by thinking about her son that she was able even to grasp the concept of love. Love wasn't about feeling at ease with someone, or bubbling with happiness as a result of just being with them. Love was when you felt compelled to expend every effort to see that they enjoyed their time in your company. In a sense, the time she spent with Osamu was fairly agonizing for her. He would stay one night and leave the following evening, and if he smiled once during that time, she would feel that she'd accomplished something of vital importance. Osamu's was a strictly conservative temperament. He would meet his mother at the ticket gate in the station, walk with her through the arcade to MOS Burger, play the video game at Kiddy Kastle, have her buy him a new computer game and three volumes of various manga, ride the bus to her housing complex, hopscotch with rigorous precision over the flagstones, play the new computer game in her third-floor condo, read his manga after dinner, get in the bathtub at exactly eighteen minutes past the hour, and go to sleep holding his mother's hand. The two of them didn't do a lot of actual talking, but Osamu would always smile at least once. Tomiyama Midori would be on edge until he did, however, and sometimes it wasn't until he was on the train platform to head back home.

On this particular day, Osamu smiled just moments after they met. At Kiddy Kastle, Tomiyama Midori copied down the names of all the players who'd scored more than three hundred thousand points. In accordance with the strategy she and the other Midoris had jointly devised, she told the manager of the store that she worked in the marketing department of a major video game manufacturer and wanted to contact the high scorers and ask them to try out a new shooting game. "Could you possibly give me their addresses?" she asked him.

"Don't know their addresses," said the manager, whose face was like a squashed orange. "But I got a list where they go to school."

There were seven names:

Shinkai Yoshiro, Sakuragi Middle School, second year
Sakai Minenori, Chofugaoka Elementary School, fifth year
Sakuma Toshihiro, Shimofuda Elementary School, sixth year
Naka Atsushi, Nishiboshi Middle School, first year
Sugioka Osamu, Koganei Electronics Institute
Fujii Masatsugu, Shimofuda Elementary School, sixth year
Maeda Takumi, Yamanobe Middle School, third year

It bothered her a bit that the given name, Osamu, was the same as her son's, but Tomiyama Midori felt there could be no mistake. She drew a star next to Sugioka's name. He had scored 370,000 points. "That guy's awesome!" Osamu said, and smiled once again. Tomiyama Midori patted his head.

Sugioka didn't notice that he was being tailed by two inconspicuous Aunties as he came out the front gate of the electronics institute. The sun was shining for the first time in many days, and he giggled meaninglessly as he sauntered along in the thick shade of the old cedars that lined the street. Following him at a distance were Iwata Midori and Henmi Midori.

"I thought he'd look like more of a degenerate."

"Did you see those bangs? I suppose there are girls who think that's cute."

"It seems his name is the same as Tomii's son."

"She said she was absolutely certain this was the one, right?"

They might have been two perfectly average housewives discussing their children's entrance exams, so much a part of the scenery that no one would have looked at them twice. From their position behind Sugioka, they couldn't see that he was grinning moronically. He was remembering the last party, at which, while everyone was laying waste to the beef jerky and dried squid and macaroni salad and pork dumplings, he had stood up and announced what he'd done, instantly becoming a hero and lifting the mood of the room to a fever pitch. "You probably won't believe this," he'd said as he placed on the table a newspaper clipping with the headline "RANDOM MURDER." He then produced the commando knife, which hadn't been cleaned and was still crusty with dried, blackened blood. "This is the blade that slit that Oba-san's throat," he said, adding with a high-pitched laugh, "The actual murder weapon."

No one doubted him. They knew that Sugioka always carried knives and liked to stab things. This, however, was something else altogether. Ishihara was particularly impressed. Envisioning the Oba-san's throat opening like Pac-Man's mouth, he realized now what his original anxiety had been all about, but not knowing how to express this he merely mumbled, "Well, I'll be," and squirmed on his cushion, gurgling with laughter. The others weren't sure how to react at first, but when Yano, whose only thought was that Sugioka had totally succeeded in abandoning something, burst out with a cackle like that of a crazed Vietcong soldier exiting a spider hole in full attack mode, Nobue too began chortling and clapping his hands, saying, "That's incredible! So you're a murderer!" Sugiyama lowered his eyes and muttered, "Maybe it's time for me to do something with my life too," finishing off with a chuckle like part of the syllabary—*ka, ki, ku, ke, ko!*—and fashion-conscious Kato gazed at Sugioka with eyes so wide they were nearly round and cried, "Now, that's what I call STYLIN'!" And for the next thirty minutes or so they had exchanged no more words but lots of stunned looks and sporadic bursts of uncontrollable laughter. Now, as he walked down this tree-lined street, Sugioka was remembering that laughter, and sniggering to himself. He recalled with special fondness the question someone had posed when the laughter had subsided somewhat—"So, like, what sort of Oba-san was it?"—and how everyone had focused on him as he told his tale.

"Well, you know, after we did the Pinky & the Killers show,

I'm kind of embarrassed to say it but I was so excited I couldn't sleep, so I took a bunch of sleeping tablets I'd bought from some street kid in Shibuya, but even then I couldn't sleep, and in the morning, you know how it is on mornings like that, you get a hard-on so bad it hurts, and I went out on the street with mine, carrying this knife with me too, which now makes me think that right from the start I was planning to take somebody down— yeah, not kill 'em but take 'em down, that was the feeling—and I saw this Oba-san in a white dress come out of the rear entrance to Ito Yokado, a white dress that looked like it was made out of jizz, and she smelled like shellfish too."

"*I* instinctively understood that this Oba-san was the one I needed to take down, and I'll tell you why I knew. It's because I'm a *hunter*. Not that I've ever done any actual hunting per se, but I read this book by a guy who calls himself Japan's Number One Hunter, and this guy, normally he works in a little advertising agency as a whaddayacallit, a copywriter, and his wife left him and he doesn't have much money and lives in Tama New Town, and he drinks a lot and gets into fights, and even though he always loses he still thinks of himself as the Number One Hunter in Japan, whether or not he's ever actually bagged any game, which he hasn't, by the way, but anyway I read this book he wrote, and when you read it you're like, *Now*, this *is a true hunter*, because this guy, in his mind he's always got a shotgun with him, even though he doesn't really have one because he failed the written exam for the license, which is multiple choice and, like, ridiculously easy, like the written exam for a driver's license. I mean, the questions are like, 'After hunting or target practice, you find you have some live, unused shells left over. What should you do with them? A: Use proper care in taking them home and storing them in a safe place. B: Divide them up amongst any children who happen to be nearby. C: Heave them into the nearest body of water, shouting SCREW YOU! at the top of your lungs.' Well, this guy would always choose B or C because, see, he's honest, that's his downfall, he can't tell a lie. So, anyway, he doesn't actually have a gun, so what does he do? He goes jogging, and as he's jogging he visualizes himself shooting down all the living things he sees on the road. He started with ants and caterpillars and things, then graduated to praying mantises and cabbage butterflies, turning all the jogging courses around Tama New Town into killing fields, and then after a while he conquered his fear and started targeting dogs and cats. The way he puts it in the book, I don't remember the exact words, but it was like, 'It's not only deserts and savannas and mountain forests that can serve as hunting grounds, but the city itself. Right in the middle of the city, that's my hunting ground, and it's mine alone.' That's what he says, and then he says that survival of the fittest is just another namby-pamby philosophy that can't really help you when you're living in the city. He goes: 'What's important is humanism. We need to realize our hunting in the imagination, being true to that incomprehensible teaching known as humanism, and if possible to realize it in reality too.' Pretty cool way to put it, eh?"

As he was speaking, Sugioka looked around the room and

noticed that for once everyone was listening carefully and trying to follow what he was saying. Nobue knitted his brow—a rare sight—and said, "Amazing. He sounds like a truly amazing man." Ishihara's eyes were shining as he added, "I'll say. But this book—where can you buy it? Who's the publisher? Kadokawa, I bet, yeah?" Sugiyama stared down at his hands and muttered, "Deep. That shit is deep!" while Yano, looking like a hopped-up Vietcong fighter preparing for an attack on a moonless night, shouted, "He's a DOER, that's what he is! Not a Thinker, like that Rodin guy, but a Doer," and a dewy-eyed Kato murmured, "Now, *that's* the sort of gentleman who should carry a shoulder bag by Hunting World!" Thrilled with the reflection that this had never happened before—all eyes on one person, all ears on one tale—Sugioka kept talking.

"In other words, you visualize bringing something down, but you can't do that with just the power of your own will, you need some sort of help. Like in my case it was morning wood and not enough sleep, but it can't be something like ideas or ideology or whatever—things like that aren't worth squat, according to this guy. He says that after targeting dogs and cats and things he started visualizing himself taking down human beings, but that was it, that's as far as he went, just visualization. But then one morning who should put his teachings into practice in the real world but me? I mean, just because I came up behind that Oba-san and poked her in the ass with my tent pole, she starts screaming like a banshee. I'm not about to put up with that kind of shit. Anybody would've lost it, right? I mean, what about my dignity? So I broke through the imagination barrier and took out my knife in the real world and slit her throat, guerrilla-style, and that was it. It was the right thing to do too."

Everyone agreed. "It's true. You've got to take things to the limit," somebody said, and somebody else said, "When you come right down to it, murder's the only thing that has any meaning these days."

Such were the triumphal moments Sugioka was remembering as, snickering to himself, he reached his apartment building. Henmi Midori and Iwata Midori made a note of the address.

The five remaining Midoris gathered at Iwata's home to conduct a study group on the subject of How to Commit a Murder. Iwata Midori's three-room condo was relatively upscale but made of flimsy new "engineered materials," and the walls were so thin that the Midoris had to speak quietly and suppress the volume on the videos they'd acquired to aid in their research. Various murder methods were proposed and analyzed. In hushed voices they argued the pros and cons of poisoning and bludgeoning and strangulation, and all were shocked and profoundly moved when they realized that they were actually listening to one another's opinions. Iwata Midori was the first to remark on it. "We've never really shared ideas like this, and listened to each other like this before, have we?" she said. "I know," said Henmi Midori. "It's like, if you listen carefully to what other people are saying, you can really understand what they're trying to say, you know what I mean?" And Takeuchi Midori summed it all up: "It kinda makes you see that the other person is really another person."

After nearly four decades of life on this planet, the Midoris had discovered other people. And by the end of the evening, once they'd scientifically chosen and agreed upon a murder method, they would all hold hands and weep. For women of this particular nation, who had basically never known anything beyond the Banzai Charge, it was a transformative and revolutionary night.

"The most important thing is to make sure we don't get caught."

Sugioka was grinning to himself again as he took the usual route back home from school. He stopped at the concrete-block wall in front of the Flower Petal Women's Junior College dormitory, where he liked to urinate. A wide street led to the dormitory but dead-ended at this wall, so cars were few and far between. What's more, at three or four in the afternoon, which was when Sugioka usually passed by, most of the girls were away from their rooms attending classes. It was the perfect time and place for an inherently timid person like him to express his inner pervert by peeing in public.

"After considering all these options, I'd say we'd best keep it simple—but with a bit of a twist."

Sugioka hadn't stopped to play the video game at Kiddy Kastle that day. The only thing on his mind was the party to be held the following evening at Nobue's apartment. The thought of the last party still made him grin. He had never been the center of attention before—never once in his life—and he felt extremely grateful. *But who should I give thanks to?* he wondered, and the answer was immediately obvious. Who else but Japan's Number One Hunter?

"Chanchiki Okesa" is tomorrow's theme song, thanks to me, since Kato chose it after I played it for him. What a great song that is, practically a blues tune, a really sad song that makes you really happy, which is exactly what the Number One Hunter in Japan is all about, joy in the midst of sorrow. I think I'll start jogging too, buy some jogging shoes and run through this rotten, dying town looking for game. Everyone agreed that murder was where it's at, first time we all agreed about anything, except maybe that woman with the unbelievable body, but how awesome would it be to do her just like I did that clam-smelling Oba-san? Can't do it alone, though, I'll need everyone's help. It'll be a bonding experience, and what's more important in a man's life than cementing the bonds of friendship?

"*It's* essential to maintain a certain distance from the target too, right? He is a man, after all, and if you get too close you run the risk of being overpowered."

Might as well take a piss while I'm here, who's gonna stop me, that ugly, ghost-white, sick-ass-looking junior college girl who acted all shocked when she saw my weenie the other day? Ha!

Sugioka stepped closer to the concrete-block wall and opened his fly, and he had just pulled out his equipment when he noticed a woman in a red helmet slowly driving a motor scooter down the wide street toward him. She was wearing a black vinyl jacket and pants, and a smile seemed to gleam beneath the shadow cast by her visor. The woman was Iwata Midori. She brought the scooter to a halt a short distance behind Sugioka and said, "You're not supposed to pee there." She was holding the handle of a Duskin dry mop, duct-taped to the end of which was a razor-sharp, brilliantly polished sashimi knife, and when Sugioka turned to say, "Stuff it, lady," the gleaming blade pierced deep into the flesh of his throat and came back out with a slicing motion. "Take that," said a voice, and the scooter turned and was gone.

3

Chanchiki Okesa

Sugioka was still alive as the bike sped away. In fact, he lived a full two or three minutes after the first geyser of blood. *What's going on here?* he wondered. Ironically enough, it was the first time he'd ever tried to think about phenomena in an abstract way. That leaden, sleep-deprived morning, placing the edge of his blade against the throat of the Oba-san in the white dress and slashing with all the esprit of commandos in the old war films he liked to watch, then seeing the Oba-san fall to the ground—it all seemed like something from a movie now. As he remembered it, the Oba-san had dropped at a more leisurely pace than anyone in any slow-motion death scene he'd ever seen, the knife was like an aluminum-foil-covered cardboard prop in a children's play, the street less real than a middle school art-club wall mural, the little boys on the playground like hand-drawn animated figures out of the Beatles' *Yellow Submarine*, and the sun like the sun in a cartoon, with eyes and a smiling mouth. And now that the tip of a brand-new, gleaming sashimi knife had pierced the crepe-thin skin of his own throat and penetrated to a depth of nearly ten centimeters, he experienced the same sense of unreality. The blade rent asunder countless cells and hundreds of blood vessels, and it seemed to Sugioka that another, separate Sugioka was watching from some distance away as the crimson liquid, released from its normal course, issued from his neck in a spray so dense it obstructed his field of vision. This other Sugioka seemed to be laughing, saying not to take this too seriously, that it was nothing but a dream. But why was everything this time so much like that other time? Why was it that you got this weird feeling of unreality both when you murdered someone and when you were murdered? He wondered about this, trying for the first time in his life to reason. As his field of vision darkened from red to black, he was thinking how nice it would be to think about this some more, and talk about it with Nobue and Ishihara and the others, but what that really meant, he ultimately realized, was that he didn't want to die. At the very end he was seized with absolute terror, but then of course it was all over anyway.

The meeting of the Midori Society that night resounded as never before with peals of laughter and gleeful shrieks. The meeting was at Takeuchi Midori's little house, a gift from her ex-husband, on the outskirts of Chofu City. It was a tiny prefab home made of new materials, and it shone from roof to rainspouts with an otherworldly sheen, like a house in a movie set or a diorama. The ground floor comprised only a cramped kitchen and the ten-mat living room, where they were gathered now.

Iwata Midori had been given the seat of honor, and was comfortably elevated on three cushions, with an abundance of delicacies and drinks before her. The others bowed to her repeatedly, laughing and chanting, "Wataa-sama, Wataa-sama! Lead us into the Light!" and passing around the bottles of Château Latour 1987 and Chablis Premier Grand Cru they'd pooled their money to buy at a ritzy shop called Seijo Ishii. They all laughed until tears rolled down their cheeks. Astonishingly, their old habit of rambling on separately about unrelated topics was no longer in evidence; they were actually conversing.

Suzuki Midori took a swig of chablis straight from the bottle. "Wataa, seriously," she said, "was this Sugioka creep really in the middle of taking a leak when you did him?"

Iwata Midori slurped up the slice of smoked salmon dangling over her lower lip, as if retracting a second tongue, and said, "How many times are you going to make me go over this? He had just opened his zipper and was taking out his thing, which was nothing to write home about, believe me, but, well, not that bad. . . ." A blush mantled her cheek. "So it's not technically correct to say that he was in the middle of a leak. The pee didn't come squirting out until just after I stabbed him with the Duskin spear."

Henmi Midori, already red in the cheeks from the Château Latour, flushed a deeper red. "And did he . . . I mean, you know what they always say about prisoners who are hanged. . . . That it swells up when they . . ."

My! Hemii! I don't believe it! What a thing to say! And on a night when a promising youth just lost his life!

They all leaned back and roared with laughter. Iwata Midori, with unflappable aplomb appropriate to her status as the star of the evening, fanned herself with a regal handkerchief and said, "If I had been looking down there I couldn't very well have pinpointed the carotid artery like Tomii taught me. I needed all my concentration."

"Concentration . . ." Tomiyama Midori breathed the word like a sigh, her crow's-feet twisting until they resembled the contour lines on a topographical map. "You don't know what that word means to me. I've always had this image that one day someone—one of my friends—would speak that word while I sat there beside her with a dreamy look in my eyes. Now I feel like it's finally happened. . . . This is a great victory."

Iwata Midori closed her eyes and nodded deeply any number of times.

"You're so right," she said. "Concentration isn't something women our age are familiar with, unless they follow some religion or whatever. I'm not even sure most women understand the meaning of the word. . . . But you should have seen the way I was dressed!"

Takeuchi Midori crunched a slice of grilled stingray fin between her teeth and said, "Did my Janis run well for you?"

Iwata Midori reached for a slice of her own.

" 'Janis'?" she said.

"My scooter."

"So I gathered, but why 'Janis'?"

"I used to really like Janis Ian."

WAH! Me too! Me too! Really? You too? Yes! I forget the titles, but she had a lot of sad songs, right? *I'm ugly and maybe no one will ever love me but I know the true value of love,* or *I tried to make a boy notice me by pretending to call another boy, but I wasn't fooling anybody*—songs like that. She was so good at expressing the psychology of the average girl who doesn't stand out. . . .

The Janis Ian symposium continued for some time. They were all getting seriously drunk when Iwata Midori muttered, "I thought I looked like the Moonlight Rider."

None of the others knew who this early TV hero was, but they all laughed.

"I was wearing the sunglasses and everything."

When everyone had assembled at Nobue's apartment and Kato reported the murder, saying that according to the evening news Sugioka had "died of a stab wound to the throat," no one knew how to react. They resorted as usual to mindless laughter, but for once it felt and sounded strained. Everyone noticed this, but Ishihara and Nobue were the most sensitive to it. Nobue forced himself to stop laughing with a sudden, mournful, *Ohhh,* and made an extraordinary face—one that might have caused an impartial but morbidly depressed observer to finally end it all. Ishihara managed to stop laughing only by opening his already large eyes as wide as he could, stretching to the limit the skin and muscles around them and exposing a bloodshot-red Pollock-like pattern on the bulging sclera, making a face that might have given an impartial but acutely manic observer a terminal case of the giggles. But when the other three saw these faces, they gasped, swallowed, and fell silent.

"Fools!" shouted Nobue, following the remark with a line he'd never uttered before in his life: "This is no time for laughing!"

No one thought to ask any constructive questions, such as who might have killed Sugioka, or why; nor did any of them realize that it was simply their own sorrow and rage that had stifled the laughter. It was the first time any of them had experienced these emotions. Some part of Nobue's unconscious was making an effort to find the proper facial expression for sorrow and rage, but owing to inexperience all it came up with was a sort of vermiculation of the facial muscles. Ishihara happened to see this and, to keep from bursting into laughter again, burst instead into song. He sang "Chanchiki Okesa," which Kato had suggested as the theme song for tonight's gathering.

The others joined in, all thinking the same thought:

We're one voice short.

They sang "Chanchiki Okesa" for a long time, joined from the street at one point by a passing migrant worker, and before it was over they were all shedding tears. Sugioka had been merely an agreeable, lightweight, shifty, incomprehensibly cheerful, knife-loving wanker who was remarkable only for having a new

Mac and barely knowing how to use it. None of them had ever thought of him as anything other than a deviant of some sort, but now they all agreed that at least he'd had an ear for a really good song. As they sang, they did what Japanese men have done since time immemorial when enraptured with a tune, but rather than tapping ceramic rice bowls with chopsticks, they rapped out a beat with plastic forks and knives and spoons on styrofoam plates and containers. The resulting sound wasn't a nostalgic *ting ting*, therefore, but a dry, emotion-free *pash pash*, like synthesized drums. And when they'd finally finished singing, they all sat there talking about what a great song "Chanchiki Okesa" was.

"It's a sorrowful song, yet cheerful."

"It makes you feel that, even if there's no hope whatsoever, you still want to go on living."

"You get the image of someone who has to crawl to survive, but also of a beautiful bird spreading its wings to fly."

"I wonder if perhaps the most striking aspect of this song isn't its refusal to fit into any particular category. It's not classical or jazz or hip-hop or house. If anything, it's closest to salsa."

"There's something in the chorus and refrain that makes you feel that even in these difficult times, true inspiration must still exist. And yet it seems to transcend the times and to issue a challenge to us when we decline to act in any given situation."

Such was the general meaning behind various remarks the five exchanged over the course of an hour or so. To transcribe some of these remarks directly:

"I dunno, I'm like, I feel kinda sad about everything, kinda like after yanking myself off to the lady on that children's show *Open! Ponkikki*."

"If you were drinking at some *oden* stand you've never been to before, and some homeless guy comes by and sneaks a skewer of oden, and a thug with no pinky finger beats him half to death, this is the kind of song you'd want to be listening to."

"At this convenience store I always go to, in the place where they keep the tofu and potato salad and stuff, there's always three or four cockroaches running around, and if there's three of 'em I say, 'Ladies and gentlemen, YMO!' and if there's four of 'em I go, 'And now . . . the Beatles!' and for some reason every time I say that they wriggle away like sperm cells or somethin'."

"Assholes call this 'traditional music,' or even, like, 'Japanese folk music,' but really it's more like reggae or salsa, innit?"

"It'd be great to listen to this song with, like, a much older woman—you know, a 'mature lady,' like they used to call themselves in the telephone clubs—while you're boning her standing up."

The last comment on the subject was Kato's.

"Sugioka said that when he first heard this song, his father was beating the shit out of him."

This brought on a sudden silence, and they all communed with their thoughts for a while. And then Sugiyama finally came out with the question someone had to ask.

"Who do ya think killed him?"

Three days later, Nobue and Ishihara visited the scene of Sugioka's murder, where they decided, for lack of any better ideas, to relieve themselves as Sugioka had so often done. They had just pulled down their zippers when a female voice said, "Stop that!" Replying with a simultaneous, reflexive, *Hai!*, they looked back over their shoulders. Standing there was a junior college girl who might have been constructed exclusively from the more toxic components of some gastrointestinal disease. Nobue and Ishihara were both the type of men who tend to regard all females, from toddlers to great-grandmothers, as being in some sense sexual objects, but this junior college girl was a unique exception. She wasn't deathly pale or exceptionally thin or fat, she didn't have secretions of various colors oozing from her eyes and nose and mouth, and her skin wasn't coated with pimples; but an aura of disease emanated from her in a sickly wave powerful enough to have defoliated giant mangrove trees on some South Pacific isle.

"You're not supposed to pee there."

It seemed as if even her voice were sprinkled with disease dust, like soybean flour on a ripe rice cake. Nobue and Ishihara looked at each other. They were both keenly aware that something strange was happening to them. Normally, whenever they were together and had the opportunity to speak to a female, be she an oddly sexy kindergartner or a refined old lady stopping for dumplings on her way home from the temple, they tended to view each other as rivals, each suspecting the other of trying to steal her away, and to disguise that antagonism they would both laugh like idiots. This, of course, merely frightened and alienated toddlers, elderly widows, and all those in between. But now, face-to-face with this junior college girl who seemed to be made of one hundred percent disease particles, they were united in a lack of competitiveness and an utter inability to laugh. This was a woman they would not be capable of facing unless they worked together, unless they (at least figuratively) held hands, clung to each other, and squealed, *I'm afwaid!*

"May I ask your name?" said Nobue. It was the first time since his early years in grade school that he'd been able to address a female in a normal and courteous way. This surprised him, and it surprised Ishihara too.

"I live in the dormitory over there." The junior college girl's voice was neither high nor low, neither clear nor muddy, neither thin nor thick. It wasn't the sort of voice you would ever remember. But it wasn't by any means an ordinary voice. "We have a problem with people always urinating here."

In spite of, or perhaps because of, the sheer terror they were experiencing, Nobue and Ishihara had never felt or acted so normal.

"You must forgive us! But even dogs always relieve themselves in the same places, don't they? Perhaps it's instinctive."

Ishihara wondered why his heart beat so fast as he said the word "instinctive." He thought he sounded like some sort of youthful prodigy when he used such words. It may be that the junior college girl thought he seemed gifted as well; at any rate, she smiled at him and said, "I'm sure you'll be more careful next time."

Her smile was so horrifying that Nobue ejaculated a line he never would have thought himself capable of.

"Can we interest you in a cup of tea or something?"

At the neighborhood ice-cream parlor, the junior college girl drew stares from the other customers and even the waitress. When she walked inside, the temperature seemed to drop three or four degrees. Seated across the table from her in their booth, Nobue and Ishihara finally realized what it was about her face. The eyes were weird. Not the *look* in the eyes so much as the fact that they weren't aligned horizontally. When she smiled, the eyes slipped even farther out of line. This feature alone seemed to thrust Nobue and Ishihara into a different and dreadful world, and they both grasped something that Sugioka had only under-stood a moment before his death. Which is not, of course, to say that they were any more discerning or perceptive than Sugioka had been, but merely to give some indication of the magnitude of this junior college girl's face and smile and voice.

"I don't come to places like this very often," she said, and both Nobue and Ishihara thought, *Good! Best to leave a face like that at home!*

But Nobue's delight in his sudden ability to speak like a normal person was even greater than his fear. He couldn't have laughed mindlessly if his life had depended on it, but he man-aged to smile and ask, "Oh? And why is that?"

"I wouldn't have thought that to look at you," Ishihara chimed in with a smile of his own, all the while asking himself what in the world he *would* have thought to look at her.

The junior college girl beamed at them. The waitress hap-pened to catch a glimpse of this smile; her face twitched and she let out a small scream as her tray crashed to the floor and the sound of exploding glass shattered the air into jagged fragments. Swept down into a swirling whirlpool of unreality, Nobue and Ishihara were both convinced that the junior college girl's smile had broken the glasses directly, that she possessed supernatural powers.

"Wasn't there an incident at that spot back there recently?" Ishihara asked her. If she had supernatural powers, she probably knew all about it.

"Mm-hm," said the junior college girl. "A boy with a surfer haircut was peeing there when a woman on a putt-putt wearing a helmet and shades and carrying a Duskin handle with a knife attached to it stabbed him in the neck. I saw the whole thing."

The junior college girl spoke normal Japanese in a normal tone of voice. Nobue and Ishihara couldn't help wishing she spoke some incomprehensible language. Even if they wouldn't have understood what she was saying, they would have preferred her to speak Jupiterian or Neptunese or Saiyan or Namekkish. . . . She was eating her chocolate parfait in a manner all her own. After thoroughly licking her clean spoon, she carefully used it to scoop up only the drippy chocolate syrup. She then licked the spoon clean again, using a lot of wrist action, as if trying to paint her tongue with the chocolate. She continued licking until, holding the spoon up to one eye, she couldn't detect the slightest smudge; and then, carefully avoiding the chocolate this time and making sure not to touch the fruit or the colorful mint sprinkles, she scooped up a spoonful of pure ice cream and delivered it straight to her tonsils. Nobue, Ishihara, the other customers, and the waitress all observed this performance breathlessly. It was like watching an acrobat, or a butoh dancer, or the fattest woman in the world walking a tightrope. No one had ever seen another human being consume a chocolate parfait in this manner. Nobue and Ishihara were both thinking that at this rate the ice cream would melt and get all mixed up with the chocolate anyway, when a thick bundle of sunbeams, like something

out of a medieval religious painting, suddenly illuminated the
bench upon which the junior college girl sat. One of the customers gasped, an even deeper hush descended over the room, and
the ice cream began visibly to melt. Seeing the vanilla mound
surrender its rough edges from the top down, the junior college
girl emitted a sigh of either bewilderment or despair and gazed
alternately at Nobue and Ishihara, her misaligned eyes brimming
with sorrow. Goose bumps sprouted up and down their spines,
and it was all they could do to keep from wetting their pants.
Ishihara did leak a drop or two, in fact. And that reminded him:
hadn't this junior college girl just described Sugioka's murderer?
Nobue was watching in a dazed sort of way as the girl suddenly
changed tactics and began mashing the chocolate parfait with
her spoon and shoveling the resulting mush into her mouth,
making it disappear with remarkable speed. He was thinking it
would be better for all concerned if she just took the weirdness
to its natural extreme and shoved the mess up her nostrils, when
Ishihara nudged him in the ribs.

"Hey, Nobu-chin."

He snapped out of his chilling reverie. "What is it, Ishi-kun?"
The sensation that his back had turned to chicken skin was all
but unbearable, and it was only by a tremendous force of will
that he managed to keep from climbing on Ishihara's lap.

"Wasn't this person just saying something about Sugioka's
murderer?"

"You're right! I almost forgot. Way to remember!"

"Thanks. I don't know how I did it. It took everything I had."

"To remember something so important under these conditions! You are amazing."

Hearing himself praised like this, Ishihara began making a

clucking sound in his throat. It was a sort of hiccupping spasm of the esophageal muscles that sounded like *coot, coot,* and was a harbinger of the burst of idiotic laughter that arrived a moment later. Nobue joined in. Strangely enough, the other customers and the waitress began laughing as well. Perhaps they instinctively knew that laughter was the only possible defense against the horror unfolding before them.

The only one who didn't laugh was the junior college girl herself. Nor did it seem to occur to her to wonder if all this mirth was at her own expense. She silently went about the business of demolishing her chocolate parfait.

Thanks to the efforts of Kato, who'd been closest to Sugioka, it didn't take long for them to discover the Midori Society. Each day for a week, Kato staked out the grave of Yanagimoto Midori, the woman Sugioka had killed. It was located in a vast public cemetery in Hachioji, near Kato's family home. He endured three rainy days and then three cloudy and muggy ones, during which time he completely cleared four new Game Boy titles, and on the sunny seventh day he suddenly detected a pungent smell of perfume. He saved the game he was playing and ducked down behind the gravestone he'd chosen to spy from, so nervous that he began laughing in a way that he alone was capable of, opening the mouth in the normal position of laughter but forcing the air exclusively through the nose. Nobue and Sugiyama and others had on occasion tried to imitate this laugh, but none had succeeded. The sound it produced was wet and high-pitched, like the cry of some amphibious creature, but fortunately it didn't carry.

All the Midoris were wearing suits and, possessed of the

knowledge that fragrances tend to dissipate more quickly on sunny days, none of them had skimped when applying their various brands of perfume to various parts of their bodies—hair, earlobes, nape of neck, shoulders, armpits, breasts, elbows, heels, ankles. One of them had even daubed Poison on her private parts. Iwata Midori had always wanted to try this. She had long cherished the memory of a scene from a very bad novel in which a married woman had perfumed her pubes before setting out for a secret rendezvous. The married woman's lover in the novel, she remembered, had ignited with shameless desire when he inhaled the perfume mixed with the scent of her juices. But what was the likelihood that Iwata Midori, already in her late thirties, would ever have a chance to experience something like that? She had asked herself this question many times but never found an answer—or any likelihood whatsoever—so she'd made up her mind to try it today before visiting the cemetery. *As long as I'm with my friends*, she told herself, *it's safe to be a little adventurous.*

Kato put on his earphones to eavesdrop on the Midoris' conversation via the tiny cordless microphone he'd hidden in the gravel in front of the grave. Along with the *crunch, crunch* of Oba-san shoes came a lone voice. Tomiyama Midori's opening line put an end to Kato's nasal giggling.

"Nagii! You have been avenged!"

At the party that night, Nobue announced that they would refrain from karaoke, and no one objected.

"Something huge has happened."

Having said this much, he laughed idiotically for several moments, clamping both hands over his mouth, and then asked

Kato to report his findings. Kato executed his high-degree-of-difficulty giggle before speaking. He wasn't used to this sort of thing, and spoke in an odd voice reminiscent of newscasters on public TV.

"As you are all aware, it appears that the police and the media have given up any hope of finding Sugioka's murderer. What we need most is accurate information. Please look at the materials before you, which contain data I obtained with the assistance of my Kenwood portable recorder. At the upper left-hand corner of page one, under the heading 'The Midori Society,' you will find a list of names, and below and continuing on to the next page please notice the photographs of each member of the group." He then brought his report to a close with an inexplicable, "Have a pleasant evening, and we'll look forward to seeing you again soon."

"I wonder which of these Midoris killed Sugioka," Yano mused out loud while chewing a piece of dried squid. "Not that it matters, right?" he added, and for some reason burst into muffled laughter. He was like a Vietcong guerrilla hiding in the dark, bowing his head and trying to stifle his mirth as he remembers a recent surprise attack and the unique look of shamefaced terror on an enemy's face in the split second before death. Yano continued to gurgle for some time.

"There can be no mercy or forgiveness for people like this," Nobue declaimed, adding, "What is it about this revenge stuff, though? It makes you feel all gooey inside!" He clamped his hands over his mouth and laughed idiotically once again.

Sugiyama, his eyes forming the narrowest of slits behind his glasses, gave tongue to everyone's feelings, punctuating his words with flying spit.

"In short, we can do whatever we want to them. If it was up to me, I'd take these Oba-sans and strip 'em all naked and, you know, do the sort of thing you always hear about—force a wooden pestle up their ass and piss on 'em and then rape 'em and kill 'em and shit. I think that's what we should do. After all, they're guilty of murder. Murder, my friends! We can't let 'em get away with *that*."

None of them thought to wonder how *that* was any different from what Sugioka had done.

"I think we should try to think of a lot of different ways to do it," Sugiyama went on. "Gather tips from like the Nazis and the Japanese Imperial Army and Bosnia and stuff. I mean, it's totally justified. An eye for an eye and all that—it's the only thing that *is* justified in this world. I mean, they talk about reasonable self-defense, but nobody ever talks about a reasonable sneak attack!"

Yano sat with his head bowed, snickering to himself. But he sounded strangely confident—as if he already had an answer to his own question—when he looked up and asked:

"What'll we use for a weapon?"

4

Meet Me in Yurakucho

"Buki?" said Nobue, repeating the operative word of Yano's question in the original Japanese. He shivered with excitement. "Oh, what an awesome point you raise, Yano-rin! *Buki* . . . buki . . . How that word goes straight to the *corazón*! It's like hearing Frank Nagai's deep voice played at full volume over a JBL Paragon system! Buuukiii . . . Buki, as I recall, is 'weapon' in English, but 'weapon' doesn't have the right ring to it, right?" He laughed and began humming a sentimental melody.

"'Weapon' sounds like 'tampon' or 'simpleton' or somethin',"

Ishihara said, and started humming along. The others joined in too, and soon they were all on their feet, belting out the words to "Meet Me in Yurakucho." Kato, reflecting that it was he who had triggered all this excitement with his report, took the Emporio Armani scarf from his neck and wrapped it around his head like a turban. Sugiyama put his glasses on upside down, and even the normally withdrawn Yano, thrilled that his mention of buki had resulted in such an inspired choral outpouring, clamped a large beer bottle between his legs and wiggled his ass. "Meet Me in Yurakucho" was not meant to be sung in this manner but rather in a sad, echoey whisper in a fifties-style cabaret, while beads of light from a mirror ball swirl slowly around the walls; but any pop song in this particular country, when sung by several citizens at once, tended to turn into a mindless celebration devoid of any genuine sense of melancholy.

After the final chorus, Nobue shouted:

"To arms!"

The others responded with a rousing, "Oh!" and thrust their fists toward the low, sagging ceiling of his apartment.

With Yano guiding the way, the five set off, frolicking as if on their way to a used computer blowout sale, taking the Joetsu Line from Ueno to Kumagaya to purchase a certain weapon. On the train, they played *shiritori*, a simple game in which one person says a word and the next person uses the last syllable of that word as the first syllable for a new word, and so on. Sugiyama had lobbied for drop the hankie, but because of space considerations none of the others supported him, so he went into a snit, saying that if he couldn't play his game he wouldn't play shiritori either, and sat pouting and staring out the window at the scenery. The Limited Express took about forty minutes to reach Kumagaya from Ueno Station, and in that time they managed to advance only eight words. Ishihara, who had suggested they play shiritori, said, "I'll start, then. The first word is shiritori. Next! Something that starts with *ri*." He didn't stop there, however, but began to laugh and shout "RI! RI! RI! RI! RI! RI! RI! RI!" for a full two minutes. Yano, who was next, joined in toward the end and then continued—"RI! RI! RI! RI! RI! RI! RI! *RI!*"—for another three minutes or so, laughing so hard he fell off his seat and rolled on the floor. His spittle was a fine mist permeating the car when he finally sputtered: *ringo*.*

"*Ringo?*" Nobue growled, then fell silent, and a strange tension gripped the four players. "Why ringo?" he shouted. "Why not *banana*?"† All of them laughed till fluids leaked from different orifices. Kato, who was next, repeated "GO! GO! GO! GO! GO! GO! GO!" twelve or fifteen times and then, seeing that everyone was too busy laughing to pay attention to him, began chanting the syllable to the rhythm of the train as it sped over the tracks— "GOGOGOGO! GOGOGOGO!"—finally finishing with the word *gorufu*.‡ This process had taken another eight minutes.

When they reached Kumagaya Station even Sugiyama, who had been pouting all through the commotion on the train, came back to life and began dancing about, saying, "It's the countryside! Even the station smells like country!" None of them knew what to do now, however. Intoxicated with Yano's simple

---

* apple
† banana
‡ golf

declaration—"You can buy a Tokarev in Kumagaya"—they had lost no time in liquidating all their assets and jumping on the Joetsu Line, but now what?

"Yano-rin, where do they sell the Tokarevs?" Nobue said, ceasing for the moment to jump up and down. Yano too had been bouncing around and shouting, "It's the country! Outside the station is a barbecue stand, not a Parco!" but now he stopped abruptly, extracted a notebook organizer from his briefcase, and opened it.

"Sources indicate that Tokarevs can be purchased at a hardware store near the border with Gunma Prefecture for between fifty and a hundred thousand yen."

"That's the country for you!" Nobue said, and resumed jumping. "Where else can you can buy a handgun at a hardware store?"

They climbed on a bus to take them to the border. Each time the name of a local bus stop was announced, they clamped hands over their mouths to stifle their mirth. Though the resulting, oddly metallic *ku, ku, ku, kutt!* sound they made was plainly audible, the other passengers paid no attention whatsoever to the five of them. No matter how loudly they carried on, none of these young men ever stood out, imbued as they were with the aura of having been utterly ignored since childhood.

The border between Saitama and Gunma prefectures was an inde- scribably desolate and lonely place. Kato was reminded of a movie he'd watched with his father when he was a kid—*The Last Picture Show*. He felt like he was going to burst into tears, and then he actually did. Before them was a big river with wide banks where weeds rippled in the wind, and nearby were a large pachinko emporium, a car dealership, and a noodle shop, the signs of which were all written in English. But the shape of the English script, the languid manner in which the weeds rippled, and the colors and designs of the exteriors of the buildings—as well as the cars, the tables in the noodle shop, and the clothing people wore—were uniquely depressing. *Can there really be such insidious colors in this world?* Kato asked himself in his inner newscaster voice as the tears flowed. *What paints would you have to mix to come up with colors like this, and why would you do it? Why go to such lengths to make colors that strip away everyone's courage and spirit?*

They were all feeling it. Nobue clapped a sympathetic hand on Kato's shoulder. "Let's go get that Tokarev," he said, and then, choking back his own tears, began to hum the intro to "Meet Me in Yurakucho." The scenery they walked through was horrifying. There wasn't anything to rest your eyes on. It was the sort of scenery that seemed to rip all the beauty right out of the world, with shapes and colors that robbed you of the will and energy to act. Because they were all originally country boys, the scenery resonated with them and made them glumly pensive. How was the country different from Tokyo? they asked themselves. Well, Tokyo was so crammed with stuff that it was difficult to see the reality, and more care went into choosing building materials and English scripts on signs. That was about it, they realized, but still—it beat the country. For the briefest of moments they seemed to glimpse the truth of what had made them the sort of people they were. This was expressed well in Ishihara's words as he set off walking toward a sign that read NOGAMI HARDWARE.

"It's not just that the country's boring or shabby. It's like it slowly sucks the life out of you from birth on, like mosquitoes draining your blood little by little. Heh, heh, heh, yeah."

At the entrance to Nogami Hardware was a sign in the shape of a huge hammer, and a thick old wooden plaque below it COM-MEMORATING 250 YEARS SINCE OUR FOUNDING. "They've been selling hardware for two hundred and fifty years?" Yano said. He pictured people of the sort you see in period dramas on TV, men with topknots and women with blackened teeth and shaved eyebrows, rolling up to purchase sickles and spades, and he wondered how much things like that cost in those days and what sorts of coins they used and whether they got a receipt, and if they had something like the Ag Co-op to get discounts by buying things in bulk. With all these questions swirling through his mind, he led the way inside and strode toward the cash register. The store-keeper was sitting behind the counter and looked as if he might have been there for the entire two hundred and fifty years. He didn't have wrinkles on his face so much as a face hidden among the wrinkles, a face that not even Hollywood's most advanced special effects studio could have reproduced, with skin like a dust rag used for a century and then marinated in acid. He was reading a three-month-old issue of *Central Review*, and beside him was a portable TV tuned to CNN News.

"Excuse me," Yano said to the old man. An impartial observer might have said that there was a certain resemblance between the two of them.

"Yes, what is it, the trivets are behind that shelf, the charcoal lighter fluid's right next to them," the shopkeeper said in a smooth and surprising baritone. It was the sort of voice that gets scouted by choral groups.

"Eh?" Yano wavered at the subtle but intense power of the old man's speech. "What's a trivet?"

"A trivet's something you have to have if you want to grill meat over charcoal. You boys must enjoy barbecue parties like all the other young folks, yes?"

Yano shook his head emphatically and said:

"Do you have any Tokarevs?"

Central Review fell flapping from the storekeeper's lap. His small eyes peered at Yano from deep inside the wrinkles. Then, with something like a sob in his baritone voice, he said:

"I have. What do you want one for?"

Yano's eyes widened with emotion. He opened them so wide, in fact, that some of the dried blood vessels burst with audible pops.

"You have?" he said, bending forward until his face was no more than five centimeters from the storekeeper's. It looked as if he were offering him a kiss.

"I said I did, didn't I?" The storekeeper raised his voice, spraying spittle and moving his own face two-point-five centimeters closer. "And I asked you what you wanted it for."

The tip of Yano's nose briefly came into contact with that of the storekeeper before he backed up, stood at attention, and saluted.

"We seek revenge," he said.

"Revenge, you say?" The storekeeper fell back in his chair, a deep crease forming between his eyebrows. The crease was particularly conspicuous owing to the fact that all the rest of his wrinkles were horizontal. "Against whom and why? Speak!"

His voice was even louder now, and he seemed to be getting angry—all the wrinkles were shifting toward vertical.

"Our friend was murdered by a middle-aged Oba-san, and with an unprecedented weapon—a sashimi knife duct-taped to the end of a Duskin handle!"

"What kind of Oba-san?"

"What kind?"

"The type whose husband left her and who's hurting for money but can't work in a massage parlor or soapland because she's getting too old, and—"

"According to our investigations, no. Not the type who buys her clothes at Ito Yokado bargain sales either, but rather at boutiques or specialty stores."

"Ah. So, not the sort of Oba-san who sits behind the counter at a stand bar preparing little dishes of pickled daikon strips, but the sort who puts on a nice dress and sings fashionable pop songs by people like Frank Nagai in a karaoke club with chandeliers?"

"That's correct. Frank Nagai or Nishida Sachiko or Yumin."

"And eats spaghetti with mushrooms in some restaurant with big glass windows that everybody on the street can look in through?"

"Yes, sir. Also doria and onion gratin soup and Indonesian-style pilaf and so forth."

The storekeeper squeezed his hands into fists and clenched his jaw. He looked to be fighting back tears.

"And why," he asked more quietly now and between gritted teeth, as his wrinkles ebbed and surged in complicated patterns, "would an Oba-san like that want to murder your friend?"

"The reason isn't entirely clear. Apparently she was bored."

"Gotcha," the storekeeper said, and rose to his feet. "Wait right there a minute." He shuffled into the back and soon returned with something wrapped in oiled paper, which he placed on the counter in front of Yano.

"There are ten live rounds in the magazine. It's a hundred and thirty thousand yen, but since your motives are pure, I'm going to give you a discount. Make it a hundred and ten thousand." Yano collected money from the others, counted out eleven ten-thousand-yen bills, handed the stack to the storekeeper, and asked one last question.

"Do you sell these to just, like, anybody?"

The storekeeper laughed, his wrinkles fanning out like rays of the sun.

"Hell, no. Only to people I feel good about. I like your spirit. They always say that when human beings are extinct, the only living thing left will be the cockroach, but that's bullshit. It's the Oba-san."

As she walked back to her apartment from the karaoke club, Iwata Midori was thinking about her sex drive, or, rather, wondering why she didn't seem to have one. Tonight the Midori Society had met at the usual club with the silvery microphones, and a young sales rep type had flirted with her. She had visited the beauty salon that day and taken extra care with her makeup. All the Midoris prepared in a similar manner for karaoke nights, and they always wore suits or one-piece dresses to the clubs. Iwata Midori wondered if she was the only one who felt such gratitude to the jacket of her suit. It efficiently covered her soft, bulging tummy and love handles, her dark, oversized nipples, and the three Pip Elekiban magnetic patches on her shoulders. Whenever the Midori Society met at a karaoke club instead of someone's apartment, Iwata Midori would spend several minutes trying to decide whether or not to remove the patches, which did so much to relieve the age-related stiffness in her shoulders and neck. She only went to these clubs to enjoy the karaoke and knew perfectly well she wasn't going to meet a man or anything, but— well, you never knew. What if she were to meet someone who was just her type and drink too much and lose her head and end up in a love hotel, and he, helping her undress, were to find the magnetic patches she'd forgotten all about? The shame would be unimaginable. It wouldn't simply be a question of a man she was attracted to discovering her Pip Elekiban. The shame would be in the fact that, just when she'd managed to awaken her sex drive with alcohol, the man would glimpse her reality, thereby becoming a part of that reality, and she'd have to quit pretending there was any real libido at work inside her.

But why was she thinking thoughts like these as she walked the midnight streets home? Iwata Midori paused beneath a streetlamp to take some slow, deep breaths and try to sober up. The karaoke club was just outside Chofu Station, an easy walk from her condo. The other four Midoris had piled into a taxi at the station, singing a shrill Matsuda Seiko song. She'd waved goodbye as their taxi drove off, and as soon as she was alone something unpleasant took hold of her. She called this unpleasant something "harsh reality," but of course it was really just herself. She walked down the street in front of the station and turned the corner at a narrower, darker street, on the right side of which stood the grounds of a large shrine. The streetlamps were fewer and dimmer here. She passed a video store that had recently gone out of business. Separating the shrine from the street was a narrow concrete irrigation ditch, and on her left were darkened houses. Iwata Midori always enjoyed this ten-minute walk to her condo. It was muggy tonight, though, and her underthings began to cling moistly.

She thought about the songs she'd sung, and the slow dance with the young sales rep type. Henmi Midori had shouted into the microphone, "All right everyone, it's cheek-to-cheek time!" and launched into a ballad in English—she couldn't remember the title, but it had a nauseating, syrupy rhythm—and a group of young men had approached their table and asked them all to dance. Some of the young men were better-looking than others, but the sales rep with short hair was the handsomest by far, and he had taken Iwata Midori's hand. "Waah! Wataa! No fair!" Tomiyama Midori had cried, pushing out her lips in a mock pout. The one who'd held his hand out to Tomii was young but short and hairy and puffy-faced and looked rather dense. At first Iwata Midori had stood apart from the handsome young man with the short hair, holding his hands lightly, but he knew all the right things to say. He began by asking if she came to this place often. As they conversed, he slowly tightened his grip on her hands, then slipped one hand behind her back and let it wander a little, but his face was so beautiful that it didn't feel creepy at all.

"What a nice fragrance."

"Complimenting me on my perfume—you're teasing me, right? Teasing the Oba-san?"

"Absolutely not. I don't normally care for perfume."

"Oh? Why is that?"

"My mother was a damn nightclub hostess."

"You shouldn't talk about her that way."

"I respect my mother, of course. But you can't make yourself like something you don't like."

"That's true, I suppose."

"I do like this fragrance, though. It's the first time I've ever felt that way."

Iwata Midori became aware of herself standing under a streetlamp, smiling as she reconstructed the dialogue. She couldn't have noticed Yano lurking in the shadows of the dark shrine, breathing quietly.

"What kind of perfume is it?"

"It's called Mitsouko."

Iwata Midori was a little surprised to find that she remembered practically every word of her conversation with the young man with the short hair. In her mid-twenties she'd been married to a man whose face she could no longer remember clearly. The divorce had been such a foregone conclusion that there was no way even to explain to friends who asked, "Why? What went wrong?" Not only had she forgotten what he looked like, she couldn't recall if he'd been a trading company man or a securities firm man or Ultraman or what, and couldn't care less anyway. She was unable to remember a single conversation she'd ever had with him. It wasn't that they'd never talked, of course. He was the type of man who liked to talk at noisy sidewalk cafés rather than a quiet bar or a park at sunset or the bedroom at night. He would sit in the sunlight drinking his coffee—refill after refill—and going on and on about all sorts of different things. Not inherently boring subjects like baseball or model trains or board games, but subjects that most people would consider interesting—powerful childhood experiences, for example, or the proper approach to interpersonal relationships in the workplace, or what exactly were the things that made human life worth living—but Iwata Midori, walking along this dark, empty street, couldn't bring back a single word of any of it. And yet she remembered every detail of the silly, desultory conversation she'd just had with a young man she'd met and danced with at a karaoke club. Part of it, of course, was merely a question of time. Eight years had passed since she'd split with her husband, their marriage having drained away as naturally and inevitably as sand in an hourglass, but it had been only half an hour or so since she'd permitted her dance partner a little kiss goodbye. Time was huge. In fact, maybe time was everything. Wasn't that what they always said? That time heals all wounds (and "wounds all heels")? But Iwata Midori wasn't so sure. A lot of songs too were about time solving problems or healing wounds, but the truth was that problems were solved by somebody taking some sort of concrete action, and as for wounds—well, for physical wounds there were white blood cells and whatnot. And for wounds of the heart? The only way to stop obsessing about hurtful things was to focus your energy, and your hopes or whatever, on something else. It wasn't that time did the work for you, it was just that the deeper the wound, the longer it took to heal.

If I'd been trying really hard not to forget him, I'd probably remember some of the things he said, she thought. *Or, then again, maybe not. In school I used to write down things I wanted to remember, things I'd heard or read that seemed really important, and now I couldn't tell you what any of them were. And what do I remember about all those books that made me cry when I read them back in middle school? Nothing. Words themselves aren't that important. Even if somebody says words that shock you, or make you want to kill them, or make you tremble with emotion, the words themselves you tend to forget in time. Words are just tools we use to express or communicate something. Or no, they're not even tools, they're more like means to an end. Maybe words are like money. Money's just a tool for transactions, right? What's important is the thing you buy with the money, not the money itself. So what's important about words is the thing they communicate . . . which is—what?*

She was reminded again of the scene in that trashy novel. The adulterous protagonist, before going out for her afternoon rendezvous, had sat at her dressing table applying perfume to her private parts. It was just something in a cheap, soft-porn novel, and she'd had difficulty believing that anyone would do such a thing, and yet she still remembered it so vividly. Why would she still remember a chapter out of some third-rate serialized novel she'd happened to read in a magazine long ago? *It's not about the words, but about something much stronger than words*, Iwata

Midori was thinking, slowing her steps again. At the heart of that much stronger "something" was sex, to be sure, but sex wasn't just about two people getting naked and tangled up together. A lot of other things were involved, things that make you feel so good you forget who you are, and things that feel so creepy you literally get goose bumps, and things you hold so dear you're afraid to go to sleep, and things that make you so happy you want to bounce up and down—layer after layer of things like that, all mixed up into a sticky mess with the blood and sweat and love juice. Those things got imprinted in your body—not the way the brain remembers words, but engraved or branded on your internal organs. She remembered the anatomy pictures in science class all those years ago—the reddish brown liver and red and blue blood vessels, and the nerves like tree roots, and the cells. An emotion occurred, and the nerves threw switches to alter the blood pressure and heartbeat, and electric pulses shot through the cells, so it wasn't just a metaphor—these things got imprinted in a solid, physical, biological way.

Three and a half years I was with that man, and he didn't imprint anything at all on my body. He was like one of those dolls whose tummy you press to make them talk. And the young man with the short hair? Did he imprint something?

"You're not saying I remind you of your mother, are you?"

"Of course not."

"I am quite a bit older than you, after all."

"I think age is irrelevant, in a sense."

She'd been particularly struck by the words "in a sense." The young man with the short hair looked at first glance as if he might be somewhat frivolous—interested only in things like fashion, for example—but his subtly nuanced conversation had impressed her. And she felt as if those words had indeed been imprinted on her body. Some part of her had reacted directly to them. It was similar to the sensation of someone's tongue reaching for your throat in a deep kiss, or the penis being inserted in the act of love. "Meaning" was something that entered your body.

"What do you mean, 'in a sense'?"

"I think there's either a mutual attraction or there isn't. Maybe it's chemical. Some guys like women with very pale white skin, for example, and others like a darker look. Some like serious, quiet women, and some seem to go out of their way to find women like crazed witches."

At the words "mutual attraction," her body had responded again. Now that she thought about it, though, there were any number of men who used words like that. It was because he, the young man with the short hair, had spoken them, that they'd entered her body. Having reasoned this far, Iwata Midori suddenly sensed that she was on the verge of realizing something important, and once again she stopped beneath a streetlamp. She felt that she finally understood why it was that she remembered nothing about the man she'd spent three and a half years with, locked in the powerful institution called marriage. There were things that got imprinted on you and things that didn't. These were different for each individual, but there were things that got imprinted on most people, and things that almost everyone was drawn to—the way all the members of the Midori Society were drawn to Janis Ian songs.

Something tantalizing swirled around in Iwata Midori's head, something that hadn't yet crystallized into coherent thought. It was like the little winged creatures of the night flocking to the streetlamp above her, as if trying to coalesce into a single entity.

"Well, I don't feel like anyone's ever gone out of his way to find *me*."

"I'm sure you're wrong about that. Maybe you just didn't notice."

When the young man had said this to her, she knew there was something she wanted to say in reply, but she didn't know what it was. Now, as she stepped out from beneath the streetlamp, the words she should have said came to her.

It wasn't that I didn't notice. I didn't want *to notice.*

And if, after that, she had said, *But what if it were someone like you . . . ?*

What would have happened then? She gave a self-conscious little laugh and walked on, imagining her own face as it might look if she were naked in the arms of the short-haired young man. The image was by no means unpleasant and even produced a certain dampness in the crotch of her panties, but then a series of other images followed—the strangely shaped bed of some love hotel, the cheap side tables, the hideous tile in the bathroom, the tacky curtains. . . . And in the end she decided that the young man and her own elusive libido would never have meshed. As soon as she decided that, she drew once again to a halt, her heart pounding. Wasn't this exactly what she'd been trying to get at? She'd simply never found anyone whose libido meshed with her own!

Such was the epiphany she was experiencing, when an oddly shaped black thing materialized before her eyes. It was the Tokarev, and it was in Yano's hand. *Who are you?* Iwata Midori was about to ask when the black thing spat out a short *bang*, and she felt something drill through her face.

5

A Hill Overlooking the Harbor

It wasn't as if the bullet pierced cleanly through her face. Because it was spinning like a drill, the slug pulled her whole face inward, twisting the flesh as if it were a wrung rag. Of course, Iwata Midori was aware of this for only the fraction of a second it took the bullet to reach her brain, at which point physical sensation ended. Strangely enough, however, though all physiological functions had ceased, her consciousness remained in operation for some moments. She tried to scream: *I don't want to die!* It wasn't fair that her life should end before she'd ever found an individual who could unlock her libido. She didn't waste time wondering who'd killed her, therefore, but raged against the fact that she had to go now, so suddenly, with so much left unresolved. And then her consciousness too disappeared in the milky white mist.

Yano, sniffing the gunpowder on his hand, gazed at the splattered blood and the scattered bits of bone and brain tissue for some time, then whispered, "Ready, set, GO!" and began running as fast as he could.

When he got back to Nobue's apartment with the Tokarev still clenched in his hand, Yano was humming his favorite song—"A Hill Overlooking the Harbor," which his elder sister had taught him when they were kids. The others noticed with some concern that he was still holding the gun and asked if he was sure nobody'd seen him with it. "La la la la la la la la la no worries! La la la la la la la la la . . ." Yano squeezed the words into the gaps in the melody, smiling brightly all the while. "La la la la la la la la la la la la I was going to hide the Tokarev la la la la la in my bag but la la la la my fingers wouldn't la la la la la let go so I took off my shirt and la la la wrapped it around my hand, so everything's cool la la la la la la!" He was gripping the pistol so tightly that his hand was chalk-white from wrist to fingertips. His lips were smiling, but his hair was standing on end and the corners of his eyes were twitching, as were his nostrils and temples, and if you listened closely you could hear his teeth chattering as he la-la'd. Nobue took hold of his pale right wrist and held it down while Sugiyama tried to pry the index finger from the trigger. "Watch what you're doing," Nobue said with a solemn furrowing of the brow. "If that thing goes off it'll put a hole in my new carpet. How ya like it, by the way? Bought it last week at Tokyu in case I start living with a chick. Chicks dig carpeting more than tatami, right?"

Sugiyama went red in the face with the effort of trying to separate Yano's finger from the trigger. It seemed to be welded on. "I give up," he said finally. "Look at that thing, it's like a gold-fish with rigor mortis or somethin'. It's white and cold as ice."

Ishihara leaned in for a closer look. "It's hopeless," he pronounced with a laugh that seemed to be caused by vibrations of brain matter rather than vocal cords and sounded like an out-of-tune piccolo played by a genius musician who'd finally cracked under the strain. Nobue and the others gaped at him slack-jawed, as if it had just dawned on them what an odd person he was. Between bursts of laughter so high-pitched that they played havoc with the eardrums, Ishihara now began rhythmically chanting, "Hey! Hey! Hey! Hey!" in a falsetto voice and jumping up and down to a slightly different rhythm. *Looky here*, he said.

"Looky here, I think we're going to have to cut the finger off, don't you think? Eh? Eh? Eh? Eh? Cut it off! Cut it off! Cut it off!" He was bouncing up and down the way a child might do when pleading with Mother to make rice balls instead of sandwiches for the picnic. "It's not that easy to cut off a finger, though," he pointed out. "Ever seen a Yakuza movie? Eh? There's no way you can do it with a carving knife or a Swiss Army knife or whatever. Hey! We'll need some sort of saw."

He asked Nobue where the toolbox was, then actually went and fetched a foldable pruning saw. When he unfolded it and saw the jagged teeth of the blade, his laughter edged upward in volume and pitch, and he began blinking rapidly. Ishihara's eyes

didn't resemble those of any other member of the human race—
or of any known reptile or amphibian or bird or fish or proto-
zoan or movie alien either, for that matter. His eyelids made a
clicking sound each time he blinked—at least, "click" is about
as close to the sound as onomatopoeia can get. It wasn't like a
quietly closing door, however; more like the sound glass makes
when it cracks. *Hey! Hey! Hey! Hey!* he chanted to one rhythm
while jumping up and down to another, producing that arresting
cracking-glass sound with his eyelids and laughing that genius-
musician-with-broken-piccolo-suffers-psychotic-episode laugh.

"I got a saw, I got a saw, I got a saw, Yano-rin's no Yakuza, but
watch me cut his finger off! Yay! Yay! Hey! Hey! Hey! Hey! I'm
right, right? You write the kanji for 'correct'—one, two, three,
four, five strokes—and how do you read it? *Tadashii*, and that's
my name, Ishihara Tadashi. Correct? Right! Yay! Yay! Yay! Yay!
I'm right, right? Hold him good, and I'll make like Kikori no
Yosaku: *kii-i, ko-o, rii-i, no-o*, off comes Yano-rin's FINGER!"

Ishihara seemed to be directing the words to his inner self
rather than to anyone else in the room, but the powerful waves
of energy he emitted went rippling through the others. Nobue
was the first to join in the laughter and begin bouncing up and
down alongside him. "That's right, that's right, Ishi-kun's right!"
he declared, and soon all except Yano were pogoing about the
room in agreement. The floor seemed on the verge of collapse
as they bounced and shouted, "Off with his finger! Off with
his finger! Off with his finger!" Nobue and Sugiyama and Kato
grabbed hold of Yano—who was still desperately humming "A
Hill Overlooking the Harbor," though no one could hear him for
all the noise—and when Ishihara, brandishing the saw, modu-
lated to an even higher-pitched ululation—*Hyu lu lu lu lu lu lu*

lu lu!—Yano suddenly found himself coming into contact with a mysterious, transcendent sort of power. Returning at once to his senses, he let go of the Tokarev. It hit the floor, and Ishihara said, *Oh, poo.*

"Oh, poo. You're no fun."

"When you hear the name Tokarev, you can't help but think of the former Soviet Union, but . . ."

Yano's right index finger was as white and swollen as if it had been soaking in brine for days, but he'd regained his composure. Everyone was glad to see that he was himself again—with the exception of Ishihara, who was still cradling the saw, repeating the words, "You're no fun," and pointedly ignoring whatever it was that Yano was going on about.

"I'm sure you all know this already, having read the articles in the newsweeklies and so forth, but that model was actually the T-54, manufactured in China."

Yano had begged them to let him keep the Tokarev, but Nobue and the others had convinced him that it needed to be disposed of. They decided to drop it in one of the huge dumpsters for noncombustible trash near the housing projects on the border with Fuchu City. They'd all go there together, if only to make sure Yano didn't back down.

"It's the most common handgun on the Japanese black market these days, though of course it's the first time I personally have ever handled one."

Yano had agreed to abandon the gun but was still dawdling. First he'd fooled around coating one side of it with ink and trying to print the impression on paper as a keepsake, the way some people do with fish they've caught. He had then completely disassembled the Tokarev and replaced several components with similar parts from model guns. Now he was wrapping the harmless hybrid around and around with duct tape. Yano had made an exhaustive study of novels and films in which handguns play a prominent part, and he performed the procedure with obsessive precision.

"The truth is, we shouldn't even call it a Tokarev. It's really a Black Star. The Black Star, as you all know, was first produced in 1951."

None of them had known any such thing, of course.

"The 54 was an improved model based on the 51, but because it's essentially the same as later models of the Tokarev TT-33, I suppose there's no harm in referring to it as a Tokarev, as we've been doing, but the thing about this particular gun is, if you don't put it right up to the person's temple, or right in their face like I did with that Oba-san, you're probably going to miss. Even Yakuza say they're afraid to use the T-54 because you never know where the bullets are going to go. But on the other hand, those nine-millimeter rounds are way lethal."

Yano was eating shrimp-flavored rice crackers and drinking 100% apple juice. He had finished with the duct tape and was taking a sip of the juice when Nobue, with a grimly serious squint, said, *Yeah, but wait.*

"How come that Oba-san didn't scream or try to run when you shoved the gun in her face? Most people would try to get away, right?"

Yano tilted his head to one side.

"She looked like she was remembering something," he said. "She stopped walking and was just standing there, like she'd realized she left something important behind."

The Midori Society was down to only four members now. A group of four, it goes without saying, is completely different from a group of five or six—or two or three, for that matter. The headline in the paper had said "UNEXPLAINED MURDER" and, beneath that, "Drug-Fueled Thrill Kill?" The article included comments by a source at police headquarters to the effect that, as there was no discernible motive behind the killing and no weapon or any other clues had been found, it was unlikely that the coward who'd committed the crime would ever be apprehended.

Henmi Midori's abode was the smallest of any of the Midoris', and the most modestly furnished and decorated. She rented one section of an old house that had been divided into three. The house, in one of the more nostalgic sections of Chofu, had a small garden, and the precisely fitted tatami mats conspired with the pillars and walls and ceiling of traditional materials to lend a certain calm and somber atmosphere appropriate to the evening of the day they'd said their last farewells to a dear, departed friend.

"So it's just the four of us now," Suzuki Midori said. She felt it was up to her to assume the burden of leadership now that

Iwata Midori was gone, though it hadn't necessarily occurred to the others that there was any need for a leader. The sun had long since gone down and night was deepening, but the four surviving Midoris were for once drinking only green tea, and no one had even touched the chocolate cookies or the hand-basted soy-sauce-flavored rice crackers, which lay neatly arranged on a red lacquer tray before them.

"Four is an odd kind of number," said Henmi Midori. "All this time there were six of us, and now, having this happen to Nagii, and then to Wataa, one after the other . . ."

It was a sad thought at a sad time, and yet it couldn't dispel a certain unlikely sense of optimism that permeated the room. Iwata Midori's wake and funeral had been held in her hometown in Shizuoka, so of course her remains weren't here with the surviving Midoris. But the absence of her corpse had nothing in particular to do with the air of optimism. Ordinarily, if you were quietly sipping green tea on your return from the funeral of a dear friend who'd been brutally murdered, you would experience a profound emptiness and sorrow, a fretful sense of powerlessness against the things in this world that, once done, can never be undone—but it wasn't like that for the Midoris. What all four of them were thinking, remarkably enough, was, *We'll settle this one way or another.* Perhaps this mentality of theirs was related to the one that gave rise, during the great war so far in the past now, to those famous group suicide attacks. For the Midoris, presumably, the brain circuitry that allowed such thoughts as, *What's done is done, and since we can't change it we might as well accept it,* had never existed in the first place.

"Speaking of groups with four members," said Tomiyama Midori, "you can't help but think of the Beatles."

Her tone of voice showed that this was keenly felt, but there was also a certain rosy hopefulness in the thought that helped take the edge off the others' feelings.

"So, before this happened to Wataa, I guess we were the Rolling Stones?" Takeuchi Midori said with a little laugh and a smile.

"Were there any bands with six members?" Suzuki Midori wondered, and with this, the air of optimism that permeated the room began swirling with chatter.

"I'm pretty sure Uchiyamada Hiroshi & Cool Five were six people."

"Six isn't a very convenient number for doing most anything, is it?"

"Then again, a family with four children, if you include Mama and Papa, that makes six, right?"

"When I was still married, my little boy and I set a record of five MOS Burgers between the two of us but, sure enough, we never made it to six."

"The Sobu Line used to have six cars to a train. Did you know that?"

"The Audi logo is four circles, and the Olympics is five."

"So if we were only three, what would we be?" Henmi Midori asked. "The Kashimashi Sisters?"

Being likened to a slapstick comedy trio didn't sit well with the others.

"That's not funny," Suzuki Midori snapped. She stood up and extracted a bottle of Canadian Club from the tea cabinet. After draining the remaining green tea from her cup, she replaced it with the fragrant rye, then knocked the stuff down in one gulp, like a kamikaze pilot just before takeoff. "The Kashimashi Sisters, my ass! We haven't gone through all we've gone through in our lives to end up like that!"

"Hear, hear! What would the last two be then, a cross-talk act?"

"And if we were only one . . . Miyako Harumi?"

They all helped themselves freely to the Canadian Club during this exchange of ideas. And as the alcohol kicked in, the atmosphere of the old six-member Midori Society gradually returned.

"We all know who's behind this," Suzuki Midori said. "The ones trying to turn us into the Kashimashi Sisters or Simon and Garfunkel are those cretinous friends of Sugioka."

The following day, Suzuki Midori accompanied Henmi Midori to the scene of Sugioka's murder. They were standing beneath their parasols, at the very spot where he'd been stabbed in the throat, speaking in hushed tones, when the junior college girl with the indescribably disturbing face and voice—the one who'd caused Nobue and Ishihara such distress—approached.

"Excuse me, may I help you?"

The two Midoris hadn't been behaving as if they were looking for help or trying to find an address, and they were startled to be accosted so unexpectedly—doubly so by someone with such a face. It was a face that instantly robbed those who gazed upon it of a good thirty percent of the energy they needed to go on living.

"We're f–fine, thanks."

Suzuki Midori and Henmi Midori exchanged looks. They

were both the sort of people who tend to gauge where they rank on the happiness scale by comparing themselves to others, so when they saw this girl they both experienced a sense of superiority welling up from deep inside and thought something along the lines of, *What a face! I guess being young isn't everything after all!* They soon became aware of a second, more powerful reaction, however—a sudden desire to go somewhere far, far away and fling themselves off a rock-bound cliff—and that swelling sense of superiority dissolved in their throats.

"And you are . . . ?" Henmi Midori asked, enduring the sensation that a heavy, bitter liquid was surging up toward her esophagus from the gap between her stomach and liver.

"I'm a Flo-Ju student. I live in this dormitory."

The junior college girl's voice made every hair on their bodies stand on end and quiver. Their pubic hairs, and even the freshly shaved stubble under their arms, seemed to wave and ripple in a hideous breeze.

"Flo-Ju?"

Suzuki Midori thought maybe the word was student slang for dripping snot or something. The girl's nose wasn't actually running, she noticed, but on a face like this a bit of dripping snot—or even dripping tears or dripping poop or dripping menstrual blood—could only have been an improvement.

"Flower Petal Junior College, we call it Flo-Ju for short, but I have another aspect to my identity, which is that I'm also a witness."

The junior college girl puffed out her chest in her white cotton blouse. A tepid wind began to blow and a shadow suddenly blocked out the sun that had been shining merrily all day.

"Witness?" the two Midoris squeaked in unison. The tips of their pubic hairs continued to undulate sickeningly as a feverish sort of chill shuddered through them, like the prelude to an eruption of foul-smelling secretions from every pore.

"Don't you remember? A while back, right about there, where you're standing now, a young man with everything to look forward to in life was murdered, and I saw it all. And then after that I was honored to cooperate with the police in their investigation, and later I met two of the victim's friends and went with them to an ice-cream parlor, where we had the opportunity to discuss various topics of interest to young people like ourselves."

As the junior college girl spoke, Henmi Midori, whose bushy area was still billowing like the grassy meadow where Nausicaä of the Valley of the Wind lies sleeping, began to feel as if the creepiest man in the world were licking her all over. But she screwed up her courage and croaked:

"His friends?"

"Such funny, cheerful boys, and the short one gave me his telephone number, and maybe I'm just a coward but I still haven't called him yet."

Don't do it—all the optic fibers will disintegrate at the sound of your voice, Suzuki Midori thought as she asked, "Do you happen to know the young man's name? We're friends of poor Sugioka-kun's mother—the boy who was murdered?—and she wants to put together a memorial album of his life."

"Ishihara-san," said the junior college girl, with a sparkle in her misaligned eyes.

Suzuki Midori riffled through her Louis Vuitton personal organizer. She found a blank page and with a pencil wrote the name in katakana:

イシハラ

"Do you know the kanji?" she asked. "*Ishi* like 'stone' and *hara* like 'field'? And if you could give me his phone number too—after all, we won't be able to contact him if we don't have his telephone number, isn't that so?"

"I don't know the kanji."

The junior college girl twisted the corners of her lips in what was probably meant to be a mischievous smile. It was a smile like rotten eggs and mildewed cheese and poisonous toadstools. Suzuki Midori and Henmi Midori, receiving the full impact of this smile from a mere seventy centimeters away, felt their stomachs shrivel, along with two or three other internal organs, and a greasy sweat oozed from their temples.

"You see, girls of our generation, we write boys' names in katakana, like you do for foreign words, instead of kanji, probably because a young man's existence itself doesn't mean much of anything anymore, so their names are just sounds that don't have any meaning, like Toshi-chan or Fumiya or Jun or Takashi or Takeshi or Yoshihiko or Kazu or Tomo or Yuki or Akira or Yasushi or Keisuke or Kohji or Yohsuke or Satoshi or Tohru or Yuji or Potato or Jello or Cheeto or Tofu or Edamame or

Monkeystoolmushroom or Bouillabaisse. I guess that's just the way we girls of today are."

From their temples, the drops of greasy sweat slid down the hair tucked behind their ears to the nape of the neck and around to the base of the throat, finally soaking into the silk of their blouses. This sweat seemed many times heavier—hundreds of times heavier—than the sort one produces when in a sauna or playing tennis, and it made a deep, rumbling sound as it rolled past their ears. *Another five minutes face-to-face with her*, Suzuki Midori thought, *and I won't even know who I am anymore.* The girl wasn't tremendously ugly or disgustingly unkempt or anything like that. It was just that vague asymmetry of her eyes and face that seemed to suck energy like a black hole.

"But, oh, the telephone number, it's in the drawer of my desk, shall I go get it? Or—it's only a small room, but would you like to come in? This is a women's dormitory, of course, so there's a strict rule against having men in your room, but there's no problem whatsoever with having other women visit you, especially such elegant and sophisticated ladies as yourselves. You don't look like cult members or anything, and a friend of mine who's studying in London sent me some apple tea, and I'd love for you to try it."

Before I'd sit sipping apple tea brewed by you, and looking at that face of yours, thought Suzuki Midori, *I'd strip naked before a handsome young male friend and suck jam through my nose.* "That's very nice of you," she said, "but we too, when we were in junior college, lived in women's dormitories very much like this tranquil sanctuary of yours, and although there's nothing we'd like better than to visit your room, it wouldn't be right, really. After all, a women's dormitory is one of the few truly sacred places left in this nation of ours!"

When the junior college girl nodded and trotted back to the dorm to retrieve Ishihara's number, Henmi Midori's head drooped, and she wobbled on her feet. Suzuki Midori lent her a supportive arm.

"Be strong," she said. "If we fall down now, how will we ever avenge Wataa?"

"Yes. Yes, you're right." Henmi Midori took a Chanel handkerchief from her Lancel bag and pressed it against her temples and forehead and neck. "What is she, though? Is she really an earthling, with the same kinds of genes and everything as us? When I saw that face, and heard that voice . . ."

"You lost the will to live, right?"

"Yes! No matter what anyone said, even if my spirit couldn't be reborn in the Pure Land, I just wanted to sink to my knees and beat my head against the pavement."

"I know. But listen—I just realized something big."

No sooner had Suzuki Midori said this than the junior college girl reappeared, skipping toward them with her hands linked behind her back. The two Midoris understood what it must feel like when the torturer returns with a fresh list of questions. Both experienced a wave of vertigo, and each opened her stance and bent her knees slightly, bracing herself to keep from collapsing.

Taking care not to look directly at the girl's face, Suzuki Midori copied Ishihara's number down in her organizer.

"Are you sure you won't have some apple tea?" the junior college girl said. "I've also got a pumpkin pie I bought. I was hoping to share it with somebody in the dorm, but I'd be—"

They interrupted to explain in a jumble of words that they were terribly busy helping Sugioka-kun's mother with her memorial album and goodness look at the time, and with that they spun on their heels and ran like hell. Not until they had turned a couple of corners did they slow to a stop and try to catch their breath.

"So tell me. What's the big thing you realized?"

Though she'd just sprinted a good hundred meters, Henmi Midori's face wasn't flushed but grayish blue. One sensed that if she hadn't spoken she'd have dissolved in tears, or possibly died.

"Well, think about it," Suzuki Midori said. "This friend of Sugioka's, this Ishihara, gave that girl his telephone number, right?"

"Eh?" Henmi Midori stared at her with a wild surmise. The hand lifting a handkerchief to her brow froze in midair as the look of astonishment turned to one of disbelief and disgust. "That's right! And she said they went to an ice-cream parlor together!"

"Would a normal person go out for ice cream with a girl like that?"

"Not even the worst sort of pervert would. Not even a man who'd just got out of prison after twenty years."

"Well, that proves it," Suzuki Midori said, and started walking.

"Proves what?"

"We're dealing with maggots. Our dear Wataa . . . was murdered by maggots."

All four members of the Midori Society met after work at Shinjuku Station. They took a train to Ohtsuki, whence they made their way to a Japanese-style inn on the shore of Lake Yamanaka, a place Suzuki Midori had visited several times many years before. About a month and a half had passed since Iwata Midori's funeral. Lake Yamanaka no longer buzzed with the crowds of summer, and though it was a Saturday night, there weren't many people or cars. The inn was a short walk from the place where you boarded the famous white swan paddleboats. This was the first trip any of them had taken for some time, and as they walked toward the entrance of the inn, where a sign said LAKESIDE LODGE, they chattered gaily.

"A place near the water is romantic even at night, isn't it?"

"Three years ago I came to Lake Yamanaka with the only man I ever cheated on my husband with. . . ."

"It used to be my dream to ride in a swan boat. . . ."

"Those rugby players looked like a bunch of idiots, didn't they? Jogging by all bare-chested. . . ."

They had made a reservation, and a late dinner was waiting for them after they'd bathed. At this particular inn, the food wasn't brought to the rooms, so they gathered in the dining hall at long wooden tables reminiscent of old-fashioned grade-school desks. The chairs weren't the normal pipe-and-plastic sort but those good old round, backless, three-legged stools that were never perfectly stable and tended to clatter back and forth whenever you shifted your weight. As they seated themselves, a small window behind the counter opened, and an elderly woman in an apron—born thirty years or so too soon to have been a member of the Midori Society—spoke to them in a voice like tiny glass bells, a voice that might have belonged to a schoolgirl.

"I've heated up some miso soup, so if you wouldn't mind coming up to the counter and helping yourselves . . ."

The miso soup contained potato slices and leeks, and it was

soon joined on the table by festive platters of macaroni salad, stuffed green peppers, and teriyaki chicken.

"Isn't this great?" Suzuki Midori said. "It must be ten years since I've been to this inn, but nothing's changed."

"Most places—even ski lodges—used to have this same system for dining," Henmi Midori observed, and there followed the usual gabbling babble. *Waah, what fun! This really takes me back! The green pepper's yummy! Do you think these potatoes are organic?*

Takeuchi Midori got everyone's attention by holding up an index finger. "Something's missing," she intoned solemnly. "And that something is . . ."

"Beer!" they all cried in unison.

And at precisely the same moment, a great *BOOM!* shook the earth beneath them. More booms followed shortly, rattling the empty glasses on the table. They also heard, at irregular intervals, a dry, staccato *ta ta ta ta ta ta ta!* The Midoris remained silent, listening, even after the oversized bottles of beer arrived.

"Excuse me." Suzuki Midori made a show of calling to their elderly hostess in the kitchen. "What are those sounds?"

"It's Kita-Fuji," the old woman replied in her young girl's voice. "There's a Self-Defense Forces training area there, you know, on the north side of Mount Fuji. Nighttime artillery drills."

Suzuki Midori turned back to the others and said, "You see?"

All of them nodded. They saw.

6

Rusty Knife

"I told you. This area has always been popular with young couples and all that, but not many people know that it's also a treasure trove of weapons."

Suzuki Midori poured herself some beer from one of the big bottles as she said this, not forgetting to tilt the glass to stifle the foam. Ever since Iwata Midori had taken the bullet that made such a mess of her face and robbed her of her life, Suzuki Midori had gradually assumed, if only tacitly, the role of leader, and now the other Midoris followed her example by filling their own glasses as well. To pour one's own drink was contrary to custom, and all four of them exchanged glances, fully aware of the significance of their break with convention. It was a bold expression of the plain fact that none of them had a special someone in her life to pour for her, or for whom to pour. This was something they'd never thought about when they were six. Whenever they'd gathered at someone's apartment or condo in those days, they had always poured for each other in a random sort of way, saying things like, *You'll have some more, won't you?* or *Allow me!* Three of the surviving Midoris worked in business environments, and they all knew that in Europe and America it was common for gentlemen to pour for ladies and for the host of a party to pour for each of his guests—especially when fine wines were involved. Further complicating the matter was the fact that recently in their own country there had been incidents in which certain business executives, who'd insisted during company R&R trips that female employees pour the drinks, had been sued for sexual harassment. In any case, it was decidedly not in a spirit of loneliness that each of the four surviving Midoris poured her own beer and watched the others do the same.

"Well, then," Suzuki Midori said, and they raised their glasses.

Since the deaths of their two comrades, all of the remaining Midoris had come to a more or less unconscious realization. None of them had ever found, aside from their respective fathers, a man who made them feel from the bottom of their hearts that they wanted to pour his beer or have him pour their wine; and now that they were heading into their late thirties it was extremely doubtful whether any of them ever would find such a man. It wasn't a question of lonely or not lonely, however.

Each was convinced that the fact that she'd never burned with passion for a man was due to various circumstances in her life that mitigated against such passion—circumstances in her family, for example, or in her social milieu or workplace or community. And they realized now that their mindless "You'll have some more, won't you?" had only served to obfuscate reality by keeping things vague and ambiguous.

But why had this realization, unconscious and unformulated though it may have been, come to them now? Put this too down to the sudden and unexpected deaths of their comrades. The two departed Midoris hadn't had the opportunity to experience such revelations, and now they never would. It was in order to honor the memory of these unfortunate two that the survivors had filled their own glasses and now prepared to drain them with quiet dignity. It had nothing to do with loneliness. All four shared an unconscious and unspoken conviction that for them, at least, certain possibilities still remained.

"*Kanpai!*"

They quietly clinked their glasses together.

"To a successful operation."

The Midoris awoke early on Sunday. To pass the time until evening, when they had an appointment to meet with a certain man, they rented bicycles and explored the roads that rose toward the foothills. Later they would stop for lunch at an Italian restaurant in the forest, a place with an extravagant interior, an impressive menu, and all-but-inedible food. Later yet they'd play tennis and then, toward the end of the day, paddle about the lake in a swan boat.

"I once almost got serious with a man who, whatever vacation spot we went to, could only think of one thing—renting bicycles. It seems like a long, long time ago now, but . . . I guess it's only been seven years or so."

The bicycle rental shop was a tin-roofed shed about ten minutes on foot from the inn. They'd found the straw-hatted old man who ran the place stretched out on a deck chair, roused him, and rented two pink and yellow tandem "Lovers' Cycles." They were now pedaling these up a narrow paved road away from the lake, where the fragrance of earth and grass wafted through remnants of morning mist.

"So you cycled together in lots of different places, then?"

"Yeah, but not really 'vacation spots' so much, now that I think about it. I guess the place that made the biggest impression on me was Canada."

"You went to Canada? Lucky you! I've seen TV shows about Canada. It's supposed to be really beautiful, right?"

"All I really saw was Vancouver. The man I almost got serious about had to go there on business, and we decided I'd visit him sort of secretly, but I could only stay three days. It was definitely a pretty place, the scenery and everything, but there wasn't much to do. Seems like all we did was ride bikes."

"Hemii, you never told us about this before! You were married then, weren't you? You mean you were having an affair?"

"My husband and I were already separated by this time, and the bicycle-lover was in the same sort of situation. Anyway, there wasn't that much you could do or see on a bicycle in Vancouver, but at the close of each day we'd end up at this little zoo. I mean, I guess you'd call it a zoo. It wasn't on the scale of Ueno Zoo or Tama Zoo or anything, but the entrance or whatever, the gate where you bought tickets, was really magical, like something out of a fairy tale, and there was a big painting of one of the animals, but without anything tacky about it, if you know what I mean. I still remember that place. Or maybe I should say, that's about all I do remember."

"What kind of animal? A grizzly bear? Or a moose or something?"

"A white wolf. This wolf was the biggest attraction at the place, kind of like the panda at Ueno, and there were usually lots of people in front of its cage, but we always got there around sunset, when most of the people were leaving. I still remember buying the tickets and going in to see the wolf, and even though I was already in my thirties my heart was pounding like a little girl's."

"Because of the white wolf?"

"That was a big part of it, yeah, though of course there was the bicycle-lover too—but the funny thing is, I can hardly remember anything about *him*. Of course, we only dated for a short time but, I mean, why is it that I barely remember a man I almost got serious about but can still close my eyes and see that white wolf so clearly? He was all by himself, because the other wolves were in a separate cage—I mean, they weren't cages so much as these fenced-in spaces that looked like mountain scenes, with big rocks and everything—and each of the three times we went there that white wolf was sitting in this very noble sort of pose on top of the highest rock, kind of looking off into the distance and not moving a muscle. I remember asking the man, 'Is it alive?' And to this day, every time I go cycling, which isn't very often because, I mean, when do you get the chance? But each time I do, I remember that white wolf sitting there like a statue on those gray rocks, and I remember saying those words. *Is it alive? Is it alive? Is it alive?*"

The Italian restaurant was nestled in a wooded area dotted with small villas and summerhouses. The building itself was unusual, in that its exterior walls were made of concrete poured into molds to resemble square, round, and triangular logs, and the name of the place was almost too long to say without pausing for breath: Monte Varvarini di Noventa. When the Midoris arrived on their bicycles they were greeted at the entrance by a foreigner wearing a threadbare tuxedo and bleating, "*Irasshaimase!*"—not an Italian man, apparently, but one from the Middle East or South America or someplace. They ordered spaghetti and carpaccio and minestrone and linguine. The fact that there were no other customers in the restaurant made it seem a sort of showcase for the bursting of the economic bubble, and the spaghetti carbonara was, to everyone's astonishment, garnished with crumbled scraps of hard-boiled eggs.

"In my office there's this twenty-three-year-old who recently got married, and she invited me to her wedding because we used to have tea together sometimes, and she always just struck me as an average sort of girl, but then the other day she called me up and said, 'Takeuchi-san, I'm having an affair!' "

"My! And she just got married, right?"

"Just a couple of months ago. But the guy she's having an affair with, she was seeing him even before she got married, and she says he was actually more her type but he wouldn't ask her to marry him, so she was like, *All right, you're not the only man in the world*, and she married this other guy she was seeing at the same time. The one she married is some sort of civil servant and very serious and conservative and when they have sex it's over before she knows it and the things he talks about bore her to death, and the other one works in a boutique in Aoyama and plays in a band and knows how to get any drug you might want, and he seems to have other girlfriends too, but she sees him two or three times a week, and then about a week ago the civil servant found out about it, and the way he found out was because she didn't know the other guy's condom had slipped off and was still inside her and her husband found it when they went to have sex, and she just thought, *Oh, to hell with it,* and told him everything, and would you believe it? He started bawling like a baby and pleading with her, going, 'It's okay if you want to keep seeing the guy, just please don't leave me!' "

A man like that, the four Midoris all agreed, had no business being alive.

After lunch they headed for the tennis courts.

They rode the tandem bicycles down a dirt road to the courts and rented rackets and balls at the little log-cabin-style office from a young man with no shortage of pimples. He directed them to Court B, where they split into two teams for a doubles match. None of them had ever played before, so their serves were rarely within the lines and nothing resembling an extended rally ever occurred, but the four Midoris enjoyed themselves immensely, cheering and shrieking every bit as energetically as the younger groups on either side of them. They had reserved the court for two hours, but after an hour of playing their particular style of tennis, in which all four players jump up and down and squeal with delight whenever one of them manages to hit the ball, they'd had their fill and sat down on the benches, drinking sports drinks and chattering excitedly. None of them had produced so much as a drop of perspiration, but they had achieved one of their dreams—tennis by the lake—and spirits were high. Tomiyama Midori peered up at Mount Fuji, looming right in front of them, and said, *Come to think of it* . . .

"I used to come here when I was little, not the tennis courts but Lake Yamanaka. I wonder why I've forgotten about that for so long. My father worked in a bank that had a lodge where the employees could stay on their holidays. Judging from the position of Fuji, I'd say it was on the far end of the lake, like if you walked halfway around the lake from here, that's about where the lodge was. It seems like we went there every summer when I was little, but of course my father was just an average clerk in the bank, so he could never get a vacation of any length, more like three days at a time, and I even seem to remember trips where we stayed at the lodge just one night, but anyway we went there many, many times. I wonder how old I was when this thing happened—I remember my father carrying me on his shoulders, so I must've been really small, first or second grade, maybe. It wasn't much of a lodge or anything, nothing special about it, just a dining hall and three or four rooms upstairs lined with bunk beds, but it was on this gently sloping hill, and out in the garden was a barbecue, just a simple one made out of bricks with a heavy iron screen kind of thing sitting on top, and I remember the last dish we'd cook would always be *yaki-soba* noodles, but we grilled all sorts of things, steaks and potatoes and hamburgers and frozen prawns, and the adults drank beer and we kids drank orange pop, and then, before going to bed, we always had fireworks. My father usually took his vacation after the Obon holidays, so it was just about the time of year it is now, but it's funny, isn't it, that I'd suddenly remember this? I had this one big firework called a Rainbow Fountain, because it would shoot out this fountain of colorful sparks for like forever, but the fuse was damp and it wouldn't light. We always started with the little ground spinners and sparklers and things and gradually went bigger and bigger, and this one that wouldn't light was the one I'd been saving for last, so it made me really sad and I started crying, and my father came up to me and said, 'What's wrong?' and I just pointed at the dud firework, and he squatted down and reached for it, and wouldn't you know, just as he's reaching for it the damn thing goes off. He managed to cover his face with his left hand, but his right hand got really badly burned. You know, fireworks are incredibly hot, hotter than fire even, and my father's hand turned all white, but he didn't want me to worry, so even though he was biting his lip to keep from screaming he tried to smile. He held his hand under the faucet and ran cold water over it, and then they put on some ointment, but after a while it swelled up to about twice the normal size. But he kept telling me it didn't hurt, didn't bother him at all. And then, years ago, the last time I remember thinking about all this, I was trying to make some porridge with this turtle soup stock that one of the girls at my office had given me, and as I was heating it up I accidentally touched the pot and burned my finger—just a little bit, but it really hurt—and that made me remember my father's burn, which had covered the whole palm of his hand, and I couldn't even imagine how painful that must have been, and yet he tried to act like it was nothing at all—just because he didn't want me to worry, right? It made me feel like, you know, like he really cared about me. But it's funny, isn't it? I'd forgotten all about that this entire time. I wonder why I'd remember it right now."

"It's because your heart is open right now," Suzuki Midori murmured, and Tomiyama Midori nodded. The other two Midoris understood as well. And why were their hearts open now? Because they were doing what they really wanted to do. Until now, they'd never known what that was. Until now, there hadn't *been* anything they really wanted to do.

"Back when I was married, I was always somewhere else in my mind, thinking about all sort of things, and now I feel like I understand why."

They were pedaling their swan boat over the surface of the lake, plowing slowly through the shimmering golden fan painted there by the sinking sun, their hair waving in the wind.

"Whenever I was with my husband, whether we were eating dinner or taking a walk, or even just talking about things, I was always thinking about something else. At the time, though, it never even occurred to me that there was anything abnormal about that."

Suzuki Midori squinted into the setting sun as she spoke.

"When you're married to someone, you talk about all sorts of things, right? Since we didn't have any children to talk about, my husband would tell me about things at the office, that a colleague of his who'd once visited us at our home had cancer, or that a man who'd entered the company the same year as him got tricked by the mama-san of some bar into cosigning on a loan and now his life was a living hell, things like that. And we had a pet cat named Fu Ming, kind of a Chinese-sounding name, who was part Siamese, and I was still in my early twenties and didn't want to be some boring housewife who can only talk about things she saw on TV that afternoon, so mostly I talked about Fu Ming, but even when we were talking and laughing about the cat I'd be thinking about something completely different. 'Today Fu Ming was chasing a fly and jumped up on the coffee table but landed on a cassette tape and slipped and nearly fell off'—I'd be telling my husband some story like that, but all the time my brain would be somewhere else, some really stupid place. Like I might be thinking about that morning, when I walked with him to the station to see him off and a tall woman in a suit passed by and he stared at her for about three seconds. I'd be thinking, *That's probably the type of woman he really likes*, and it would turn into a kind of obsession that kept ballooning, getting bigger and bigger, and I'd start to feel like I hated having a person like him for a husband. It wasn't the sort of thing I could even talk to anyone about, though, so I'd just feel sorry for myself, and it would go on like that. I'd be rehashing these things in my mind, over and over, even while I was sitting there laughing with him, telling him funny stories about Fu Ming. It was like that the entire time we were together, and finally I started to wonder if there wasn't something wrong with me, but I didn't have anyone to discuss it with, and then, after about half a year or a year of that, Fu Ming got this sickness called hydro-peri-something, where her tummy filled up with water, and she died, and after she died I didn't have much to say to my husband anymore. It wasn't because I was thinking about Fu Ming or grieving or any-thing, it just felt like my head was completely empty. I mean, it wasn't about the cat. It was about the fact that I'd never told my husband any of the things I was actually thinking. So, well, I'm the one who was messed up, I guess, but it was always that way for me. I've never known what it feels like to do something and have it be the only thing in my head. Even during, excuse me, sexual intercourse, I'd be thinking about something else completely. It's terrible, I know, and I got to hate the whole situation so much that I ended up getting a divorce, but even getting divorced didn't fix the problem. But now . . . the amazing thing is that now, everything's changed."

The western slope of Mount Fuji was turning pink and lavender in the setting sun.

"Everything's changed. . . ."

The wind had died, and the shadow cast by the swan boat stretched out across the glassy surface of the lake, heralding the rapid approach of night.

"There's a place somewhere in this world," Suzuki Midori said, remembering some tidbit she'd read in a book, "where they talk about the night as if it were a living creature. Not just that day loses its light, but that the creature called night comes and swallows everything up. . . ."

The little bar they were looking for was down a narrow lane that separated the bike rental shed from a souvenir shop. The bar, sandwiched between a noodle kitchen and a coffeehouse, had an old-timey sign hanging over its windowless entrance.

The man was already there, drinking a glass of Suntory Old with water and ice. When the four Midoris opened the door and looked in, he waved and said, "Hi! Over here! Over here!" From the top of his haircut to the soles of his black patent-leather shoes he exuded, along with a faint odor of sweat, the air of a man who had never had any luck with the ladies, just never had any luck with them at all.

There were no other customers in the place, which was furnished with only a short counter and three small tables. A woman wearing no lipstick or any other makeup except for thickly painted layers of blue, green, and brown around her eyes—a dubious cosmetic strategy—and a chubby girl who looked to be about middle school age and well below average intelligence, chanted "*Irasshaimase!*" in unison as the Midoris stepped inside.

Suzuki Midori, intuiting that no one wanted to sit next to the man, made that sacrifice herself. The man, having presumably picked out the best articles of clothing he owned without giving any thought as to whether or not they went together, wore a yellow shirt, pink-and-gray-checkered trousers, purple nylon socks, a brown blazer with black stripes, and a red silk neckerchief.

"I'm Sakaguchi," he said. He was a member of the Self-Defense Forces.

"You must be the four ladies who are all named Midori."

Sakaguchi was gulping his whiskey and water even as he said this, so that it came out more like, *You must be* gulp, *the four ladies who* gulp, *are all named* gulp, *Midori.* His cheeks and the flesh around his eyes were flushed, but Suzuki Midori knew it wasn't merely the result of alcohol. He was plainly nervous and self-conscious in their presence. They might be Oba-sans in their late thirties, but this man had probably never in his life been surrounded by four women before, and certainly not by four women who had any sort of interest in him. All of them could sense that much.

"Would you like something to drink?" He arranged his mouth in a smile as he said this. "When I say 'something,' I mean whiskey, is what I mean. That's all there is in this joint."

It was an appalling and alarming smile.

"This whiskey, in the old days they called it 'Dharma.' Isn't that funny? Dharma. They used to sell it in a wooden case, six bottles to a case. From the time I was in high school I used to think that was something really special, and I decided that someday I'd become a man of such importance that people would bring me gifts like that, whole cases of Dharma. But then at some point—and just overnight, really—along come your Early Times and your Jim Beam and your I. W. Harper, and before you're even used to the idea that there's so many different types of liquor in the world, everybody stops drinking domestic whiskey. Okay if I mix it with water? This bar, the one thing about it, the water's delicious. There's a well out back, and I'm told that the mama-san and her daughter draw fresh water from it every day. Not with a motorized pump either, but with a pulley and a bucket on a rope, just like in the old days."

A lot of effort was clearly going into maintaining the smile, and yet you sensed that if you were to praise it as lovely or charming, the owner would continue to bear it for an hour or two or, if necessary, all night long. "Whiskey and water would be wonderful," said Suzuki Midori, and Tomiyama Midori smiled and nodded, saying, "We're not so young that we don't have fond memories of Suntory Old!" Reassured, perhaps, Sakaguchi finally let go of the smile. Even the mama-san and her hostess offspring breathed a sigh of relief from behind the counter as the smile was disassembled, and the Midoris were aware of tension going almost audibly out of the room, like air escaping a balloon. None of them had ever before met a man who could create a general atmosphere of panic simply by smiling.

"I heard all about you ladies," Sakaguchi said, his face back in neutral now. The Midoris drained their whiskeys and water.

"Is that so?" Henmi Midori smiled politely. "Well, a certain person told us about you too, and this bar, and what time we could find you here."

The "certain person" she referred to was a small man of indeterminate age who looked like an adult version of a premature baby and whom one of Henmi Midori's coworkers had met in a nightclub. The man, according to his own account, had started a children's clothing company some twenty years before, but after it had gone belly-up some three years ago, he'd begun working in his present capacity as an agent and go-between. Henmi Midori and Suzuki Midori had gone together to meet him in the lobby lounge of one of the high-rise hotels in West Shinjuku. The small man showed up wearing a unobtrusive suit, and as he sipped at a cup of tea with milk, he slid a memo pad across the table and said, "Write down what it is you want." Henmi Midori did as instructed and slid the pad back to him, along with an envelope containing his fee. The fee was 250,000 yen, not including the price of the tea.

"The merchandise is in the car," Sakaguchi was telling them now. "I'll hand it over to you later on, but first I need to explain some things."

After saying this much, he suddenly lowered his eyes and

bit his lip. It was as if he wanted to say something but was too embarrassed. Henmi Midori hurriedly said, "Oh, don't worry— we have the cash right here," but Sakaguchi looked up, shaking his head. *It ain't that*, he said, slipping into some sort of regional accent.

"I was contacted about this a week ago. I only had a few M16s in stock, so I had to do some real scrambling to find what you wanted, and that kept me so busy that I didn't give it any thought at the time, but then as I was waiting for you ladies tonight it hit me, and it was kind of a shock."

He looked to be on the verge of tears, and Suzuki Midori asked, "What is it?" in a tender voice, as if she and this SDF man, who looked roughly her age, were old and intimate friends. It wouldn't do to have him getting all shocked and unstable on them now—they hadn't received the merchandise yet, and they needed him to teach them how to use it. At the same time, she couldn't help but wonder what exactly it was that emanated so powerfully from men who have no appeal for women. It was almost like an odor, and it was the same no matter where they lived or how old they were or what they did for a living. Maybe you could find out exactly what it was if you did a chemical analysis of their hair or urine—discover some kind of marker that was either caused by or responsible for their never having received a woman's affection.

"The fact is, about ten years ago, I met a lady named Midori on the shore of that lake out there, and your names are Midori, and I don't know if it's karma or what it is, but this Midori, she was a terrible liar."

"My!" said Takeuchi Midori, letting this most common and versatile of interjections escape her parted Chanel-red lips, along with a little sigh. Sakaguchi seemed to gain courage from that "My!" and as he mixed and guzzled an even stronger drink he muttered, as if to himself: *That's right, that's what she was, a liar.*

"We were only together for half a year or so, but one lie I'll never forgive her for was, I was born in the mountains and never ate much fish, so I had no idea that the head of the *buri*, the mature yellowtail, is one of the most delicious parts, and a member of my squadron who was from Kyushu, he wanted out of the Forces because he was getting married—why that's a reason to quit the Forces is a mystery to me, but a lot of the younger fellows are like that these days—and I helped him out by putting in a good word here and there, so when he got back to his home town he shipped me a whole buri, packed in ice, you see, and me and some of the other fellows were talking about how to go about cooking and eating it, and I was going out with that woman then, and really enjoying every day, you know, living life to the fullest, and she came by and saw the fish and said, 'Well, first of all, you don't need the head, right?' And she cut off the head and wrapped it up and took it away. Then later I found out that the head is the tastiest part, and you use it to make a dish called buri-daikon, and after that the other fellows started calling her the Buri Burglar. That wasn't all, though. She told me a lot of other lies too."

Takeuchi Midori breathed another "My!" and gave him a melting, sympathetic look. "That's terrible!"

Sakaguchi mixed himself a fresh one, going easy on the water, and tossed it down.

"But the worst lie of all," he gargled, leaning forward with outspread hands, as if begging for mercy, tears forming in the corners of his eyes. "She told me she was a stewardess, and she was really just a *tour bus guide!*"

Each of the four Midoris made use of the interjection "My!" to convert their spasms of laughter into scandalized gasps, and they all nodded in frantic agreement when Takeuchi Midori cried, "It's just plain wrong to deceive people that way!"

"This Midori woman, I know now that she had other men, and she only came to see me when she felt like it, on nights when she couldn't meet any of the others, but what made me really angry—well, there were lots of things that made me mad, but after I realized that she probably boiled that head with daikon radishes and ate it with another man, well, I not only couldn't eat buri anymore, I couldn't eat radishes either! Also, she was a really good singer, and just because she knew I'd never been on an airplane, she told me that stewardesses have to sing for the passengers!"

The Midoris were compelled to ask a question or risk being reduced to convulsive giggles.

"You really never flew in a plane before?"

"Dozens of times during parachute training, but that was on military transport planes. But the thing that still bothers me the most is . . . is she . . . she used to tell me I was a good singer too. Naturally I started to wonder if that wasn't just another lie, and, well, I haven't been able to sing ever since. So . . . would you mind if I sang a song right now?"

Oh, please! Please do! Please sing for us! We love listening to men sing!

The song was the late Ishihara Yujiro's "Rusty Knife," and Sakaguchi's singing was so bad that it gave the lyric a strange new pathos and poignancy. Listening to his version, Suzuki Midori was reminded that no one ever said it would be easy to go on living in this world; Takeuchi Midori pondered the noble truth that nobody's life consists exclusively of happy times; Henmi Midori vowed to remember that it's best to keep an open heart and forgive even those who've trespassed against us; and Tomiyama Midori had to keep telling herself that hitting rock bottom is in fact the first step to a hopeful new future. Sakaguchi was gripping the mike in both hands, his eyes were closed, and sweat dripped from his forehead as he sang all three verses and choruses to the bitter end. The freakish mother-and-child duo behind the counter stood at attention, watching Sakaguchi's performance through eyes that shone with a mixture of unnatural fervor and bottomless despair, like members of the Housewives' Civilian Defense Corps seeing off a squadron of young kamikaze pilots.

By the time Sakaguchi had finished, the Midoris were all perspiring profusely beneath their clothing.

"Here she is," Sakaguchi said, taking a large tennis bag from the trunk of his car and casually extracting something that looked like a telescope and was only a little longer than a tennis racket.

"It's called your M72 LAW, which stands for Light Anti-tank Weapon. Comes loaded with a sixty-six-millimeter HEAT rocket. Exceptional killpower, and it's lightweight, so even a lady can use it. Disposable type, good for a single use only. The American forces accidentally left a pile of these behind after the joint maneuvers a couple of years ago. It's been properly maintained, and I think it's your best bet."

7

After the Acacia Rain

The Midori Society didn't leap into action the moment they'd got their hands on the rocket launcher but began holding a new series of study groups to research guerrilla and terrorist tactics. All four of them had regular jobs, so the meetings had to be held at night. Meanwhile, they continued to track the movements of the enemy camp, conducting regular surveillance on Ishihara, Nobue, and the others.

Saturday night, another study group. Suzuki Midori's apartment. Only three of them were present, as Henmi Midori was busy staking out Nobue's building.

"All right, then. Does anyone have any questions or opinions about the things we went over last night?"

Chairwoman Suzuki sipped her green tea and looked at Takeuchi and Tomiyama in turn. They had all decided to refrain from drinking alcohol at these meetings. Especially on Saturdays, when the meetings often lasted into the wee hours, alcohol would only invite drowsiness and impede concentration.

Takeuchi Midori raised a hand. "I'm reading the greatest book!" she said. She was drinking a cup of thick espresso, which she'd brought in her own thermos. "It's by this famous general from the Republic of Korea named Paik Sun-yup, and it's called *Anti-Guerrilla Warfare*. Three nights ago we talked about *Guerrilla Warfare* by Ernesto 'Che' Guevara, right? Well, Che's book is a sort of manual written from the guerrilla's point of view, of course, but Paik Sun-yup writes from the other side. He was a specialist in suppressing communist guerrillas from North Korea. And he—"

Suzuki Midori interrupted her. *Hang on a second*, she said.

"Takee, are you using less makeup than usual? You're not even wearing any lipstick."

Takeuchi Midori blanched and gave a little gasp. Her hand darted into the purse beside her, and in less time than it takes to say so, she was checking her face in the little round mirror of her compact.

"I'm sorry," she said with honest contrition. "I didn't realize . . ."

"I'm not saying it just to get on your case, believe me."

Suzuki Midori took a leisurely sip of her green tea. She'd

recently acquired a keen appreciation for how economical tea
and coffee were compared to things like brandy and wine and
whiskey. In the past, she had often mindlessly gulped down wine
that cost five or six thousand yen a bottle at Seijo Ishii, whereas
a hundred-gram bag of even the finest green tea from Yame or
Uji was under three thousand yen and would easily last ten days.
Besides, the caffeine kept you sharp. Leaders of all the world's
guerrilla and terrorist groups have said to drink tea rather than
wine, and now she understood why.

"I've made the same sort of mistake myself any number of
times and had to hurry into the nearest powder room to fix
it, so I'm just speaking from experience. Didn't Guevara and
Marighella both emphasize this very point: that if something's
important, it's worth rehearsing and reiterating again and again?
That's why I keep harping on these things. Going light on the
makeup is a habit you can fall into without even realizing it, but
people around you are quicker to notice such things than you
might imagine. The last thing we want is for people to think
there's anything suspicious about our behavior, right? That's
why, even though we've all got so much else to do with our time
these days, we keep meeting once a week at the karaoke club in
front of the station, and that's why when we buy these reference
works, each of us goes to the trouble of traveling to bookstores
in distant towns, putting on aprons or dressing in college-girl
fashions, or wearing other things we'd never really wear, like
those purple jeans of mine. These are the kinds of details we
have to keep working on, never letting down our guard. After
all, a group of women our age buying manuals on guerrilla warfare and terrorism at their local bookstore would be pretty conspicuous, right? Didn't Marighella and Action Directe's Nathalie

Ménigon both warn against exactly that sort of thing? We've lost two of our comrades, Nagii and Wataa, so we have to make sure there's no trail of evidence leading back to us when we exact revenge on the dirtbags responsible."

Takeuchi Midori was nodding in agreement as she peered into her compact and carefully applied her red Chanel lipstick. "How's this?" she said when finished. Given the thumbs-up, she smiled and said, "I've got to be more careful!" Perhaps it was partly because of the lipstick, but that smile was unlike any she'd ever exhibited before, and the other two Midoris were mildly stunned.

"Takee!" Chairwoman Suzuki gasped. "What is with the sexy smile? Even *my* heart just skipped a beat!"

"Seriously, Takee," said Tomiyama Midori. "Do people at work tell you you're looking especially hot these days?"

Takeuchi Midori bowed her head, blushing, and said that in fact they did.

"My section chief asked me if I'd found a new lover or something. It was strange. I couldn't imagine what he was talking about."

"You *have* found a new lover," Suzuki Midori said, and tilted her head toward the far corner of the room. The M72 was there, closed up inside its outer tube. "But back to what you were saying, Takee. What's so good about this Korean general's book? Did you find anything we can use?"

"Well, nothing in particular, I guess, but . . ." Takeuchi Midori leafed through her underlined copy of *Anti-Guerrilla Warfare*. "Oh, wait. For example: 'Japan has no history of guerrilla warfare.' I thought that was worth noting. And this one: 'A fascinating thing about human beings is that the more they begin to disintegrate psychologically, the more they tend to fall back on custom and habit.' Well, just things like that . . . I guess it's not much help, is it? No really practical tips or anything. . . ."

She closed the book and shrugged, still wearing that sexy half-smile. Suzuki Midori and Tomiyama Midori were wondering what it was that had effected this transformation in her— and, indeed, in themselves as well. They had both had similar experiences at their respective offices. *Tomiyama-san, Suzuki-san, you're looking awfully pretty lately. . . .*

It was a funny thing. Until not so long ago, the Midori Society had often taken up issues like How to Find a Good Man—a "good man" meaning one who was as wealthy as possible (if only to keep things from getting messy later on), and presentable, and who'd take you to fashionable restaurants and clubs and hotels and make you the envy of all your friends. The original six members had always shared their romantic close encounters and near misses. *Guess what happened to me! I was walking down the street today and a gentleman in a Bentley pulled up to the curb and spoke to me,* or *The other day this younger man in my office who's the idol of all the younger women suddenly came up to me and started talking about something that had nothing to do with work, and I'm afraid I got a little flustered, but* . . . There had always been plenty of stories, but in the end none of them had ever gotten anywhere in these little adventures. In those days, Suzuki Midori was thinking, it must have been as if they had the words STARVED FOR A MAN stamped on their foreheads. The funny thing was that as soon as you stop needing men, they suddenly started finding you desirable.

Some hours later, Tomiyama Midori looked up at the wall clock and said, "Shouldn't Hemii be back by now?" It was three-thirty a.m., and the windows of Suzuki Midori's living room were white with condensation. The muggy rainy season, the brutal sun of midsummer, and the hot days of early autumn were all far behind them now. It was mid-November, the time of year when a girl's fancy turns to warm sweaters and hot soups and bonfires. "She must be awfully cold, out there all night like that." The three of them sat back to drink their tea and espresso while they waited. As it turned out, the news Henmi Midori would bring would be well worth the wait.

It was a little after four when they heard a taxi stop outside. Takeuchi Midori jumped up and went to the window. "It's Hemii," she said, and the three of them went to the the front door to greet her. She looked cold and exhausted, but her first words were a breathless, "We've got 'em!" The other three insisted she come in and drink something hot before delivering her report. Green tea? Coffee? Tea with milk?

"The thing is, we can't attack them at the apartment they gather at, right?" Henmi Midori said after pouring some whiskey into her coffee, stirring, taking a swallow, and pronouncing it good. "You can only use the rocket launcher if you have twenty meters of clear space behind you—otherwise you'll blow yourself up with the backblast. So I watched the apartment tonight, just like I did last Saturday, but last Saturday, like I told you, they all got into a big Toyota van type of thing and drove off somewhere and I couldn't follow them because I didn't have a car. So tonight I parked my Accord nearby, and at about midnight these guys—'guys' doesn't seem like the right word, but this creepy group that makes you wonder how five such weird-looking characters ever found each other—they got into the van and drove off again. Well, where do you think they went? They headed straight for Izu and stopped at a place on the shore above Atami. And what do you think they did there? Get this. They put on a big karaoke show, just for themselves, in the middle of the night, in a lonely cove with a big concrete breakwater. . . ."

"*A* CONCRETE BREAKWATER!"

Suzuki Midori inadvertently launched three tiny flecks of spittle as she echoed Henmi Midori's words at many times the volume. She snatched the bottle of whiskey from the table, fumbled with it, splashed some whiskey into her cup, and drank it down straight. Takeuchi Midori and Tomiyama Midori followed suit, making it like a scene from an old western movie. Takeuchi Midori was the first to speak. Her breath was hot and whiskey-scented.

"That means we can kill them all at once. . . ."

Three more weeks went by. In the Nobue-Ishihara group, spirits were on the decline. Enthusiasm had reached its apex the night Yano reported his execution by Tokarev of Iwata Midori, and the energy of the group had been on a slow slide down ever since. The gradual advent of cold weather had played a part as well, but their last Karaoke Blast on the beach had been a listless and dismal affair, and though tonight they were gathering for the first time in three weeks, each was in his own world,

eating or drinking vacantly from his own private stash. No one
had brought much. Nobue had taken his last few cans of beer
from the fridge and set them at his end of the table; Ishihara
laid out the two jars of One Cup Sake he'd bought at a vending machine somewhere; Kato plopped down a bottle of domestic wine, a sticker reading ¥800 still attached; and Yano pulled
out a miniature bottle of Early Times. Each of them was now
consuming his own contribution, but that left Sugiyama, who'd
brought nothing, in a state of lonesome despair that expressed
itself plainly enough on his drooping face, the skin of which
wouldn't have looked out of place on a dried fish. Nobue, sitting
right across from Sugiyama with five cans of beer before him,
didn't even notice that the latter was sending him and everyone
else anguished *what-about-me?* looks as they drank their One
Cup Sake and domestic wine and mini-bourbon, and of course
it never occurred to Nobue to ask Sugiyama if he'd like a beer.
The skin of Sugiyama's face flushed salmon-pink with anger,
and he glared fiercely at Nobue for a good three minutes but was
unable to detect any glint of comprehension in the other's eyes.
He thought about kicking the table over and storming out but
quickly remembered that there was nothing to do back at his
one-room, six-mat apartment, where provisions amounted to
a sake bottle with about a millimeter of liquid remaining, two
eggs he'd bought the previous month, a jar of barley tea he'd
brewed during the summer that now supported a floating colony
of white mold, and a torn package of instant yaki-soba. He stood
up, still wearing the same woebegone expression and nodding
and grumbling inscrutably, "What a nightmare—America out
of Somalia!" as he made his way around to where Nobue sat.
"Right, Nobu-chin?" he said. Nobue looked up at him blankly

and said, "What?" And Sugiyama, with all the speed of a cockroach disappearing behind a cupboard, snatched one of the cans of beer. Before Nobue's startled "Hey!" even escaped his lips, Sugiyama had ripped open the pop-top and was noisily gulping the contents. "Mm-hm, that's right, that's right, that's right," he muttered, ambling back to his seat as if nothing had happened.

No one was putting any thought into the question of why the general energy level was so low, but it didn't help that snacks were also in short supply. Nobue had extracted from the fridge a long, vacuum-sealed, fish-meat sausage with the legend MARUHA written vertically down the length of the wrapper, an item that hangs in convenience stores like a relic of the nineteenth century, but it never occurred to him to slice it up into little pucks and hand them around. Instead, he squeezed a tip-of-the-pinky-sized dollop of mayonnaise onto one end and laughed for no apparent reason—*Ah, ha ha ha ha ha!*—before biting off about two centimeters, peering at the toothmarks in the new end of the sausage and laughing again, then carefully adding another dollop of mayonnaise and repeating the sequence. Ishihara had apparently arrived hungry: along with his One Cup Sake, he'd brought three croquettes in convenience-store packaging—a styrofoam tray sealed with industrial-strength plastic wrap. Nobue hadn't set out any chopsticks or sauce, however, and the obvious fact that one couldn't eat croquettes without chopsticks or sauce somehow failed to penetrate Ishihara's enervated brain. He just sat there playing with the unopened package, making little dents in the taut bubble of plastic wrap with his index finger. Normally even this level of mindless diversion would have triggered audible risibility, but tonight, what with his empty stomach and overall lack of vitality, he hadn't so much as chuckled. It was extremely unusual for someone of Ishihara's psychological makeup to go any length of time without laughing. Not even being beaten half to death could keep him from erupting with meaningless laughter—and this is no mere conjecture. Late one night some three years before, he'd been walking through Shinjuku's Central Park, drunk, and had jumped up on a park bench and begun singing Japanese pop songs at the top of his lungs. When he ignored the repeated cries of "Quiet!" and "Shaddup!" issuing from the darkness on all sides, three middle-aged homeless men approached, dragged him down, pounded him to a pulp, and then, with tears of rage streaming down their cheeks, made a sincere attempt to strangle the life out of him. Homicides of just this sort are not uncommon in places like Shinjuku and Shibuya, but Ishihara survived. Symptoms of cyanosis had already begun to appear on his face, in all their blue and purple glory, when he'd suddenly started laughing so uncontrollably that his startled attackers backed off. Nobue, on first hearing this story, had expressed amazement that anyone could manage to laugh at a time like that. "I don't know why, but it was really funny," Ishihara had said, and laughed again at the recollection. "There was this flood of light and sound that was like from a different world, and it cracked me up, and I figured it would be a waste not to laugh, because if you laugh you feel better even if you don't have any reason to. But mainly I just didn't want to miss a good opportunity."

Kato was eating grapes, of all things, with his wine. The store he'd bought the wine at had been hosting a promotional campaign for the vineyards of Yamanashi Prefecture, and when he paid for the bottle a strikingly unattractive young woman dressed in indigo work pants, like a farm girl from the past, had presented him with a complimentary bunch of fat purple grapes. Eating grapes with wine struck even Kato as odd. "It's a natural match, I guess," he mumbled to himself, "like corn and bourbon, or soba noodles and buckwheat gin—except those sound *good*." Yano was drinking the most authentic beverage—that mini-bottle of Early Times—but was on much less solid ground when it came to munchies. He had to make do with the eight salted beans he'd discovered in the pocket of his vinyl windbreaker, a predicament reminiscent of that of Japanese soldiers in the last days of the Pacific War. Yano thought of himself as possessing a mathematical mind, and he had removed his octagonal Casio wristwatch and was staring at the digital numbers. When exactly three and a half minutes had gone by he would make a high-pitched *Beep!* with his voice and pop a bean into his mouth, rolling it around on his tongue for precisely a minute and a half as he contemplated the salty taste, then biting into it and chewing slowly, grinding the bean into a fine mush before swallowing. At the moment of biting down, his face would relax into a smile of genuine bliss. Sugiyama was even worse off. He had nothing at all to eat. He gazed in turn at the fish-meat sausage, the grapes, the croquettes, and the salted beans and ranked them in order of desirability: croquettes, sausage, beans. He considered grapes more appropriate for dessert, an opinion he voiced in a mumbling undertone, interspersed with remarks calling for the withdrawal of American forces from Somalia, but the sad fact remained that he had nothing at all to nibble on.

None of the five thought to wonder about the cause of their malaise, much less to encourage the others or try to raise everyone's spirit. The obvious fact that the party might come to life if they pooled their money to buy a large jug of sake or a small keg of beer or a bottle of cheap bourbon for all to share, had not occurred to any of them. While none of these young men were from particularly deprived backgrounds, neither were they familiar with the concept of going out of their way to help others. They lacked the imaginative powers necessary to intuit what others might want or need, having had it impressed upon them since kindergarten that such powers were nothing but a hindrance to survival. Growing up, none of them had possessed any conceivable potential for becoming popular, and none had had even a single experience of being encouraged by anyone else. When one goes through childhood without ever receiving encouragement, one loses the ability to give it, or even to recognize it when it's offered.

Sugiyama was down to his last swig of beer, and though the poignant image of what would become of him after it was gone hadn't even formed in his head yet, he knew he felt terribly alone. His mournful eyes wandered to the window across the room, and then, suddenly, he was on his feet. "Whoa!" he woofed, abandoning the can on the table and making it to the windowsill in what amounted to a properly executed triple-jump. Knowing what lay beyond that window, the other four were close on his heels, taking their drinks and eats with them, and now all five were cheek to cheek at the window, their noses all but pressing against the glass. Through the lace curtain of the window of the apartment across the parking lot, they could make out a familiar silhouette. It was impossible to tell for sure if the woman with the unbelievable body was completely nude. She might have been wearing underclothes or a body suit or leotard, but she definitely wasn't in a skirt or blouse or trousers or robe or kimono or pajamas. "Whoa" was the only word any of them could come up with to express what they were feeling. Faintly the sound of music with an insistent beat reached their ears, and now they realized that the woman with the unbelievable body was dancing. It wasn't a frenetic, aerobic- or disco-style of dance, but a sensual affair that involved such movements as whirling in a slow circle with outspread arms, and as they drank in her languidly pirouetting silhouette, with its incredibly long legs, proud, pointed breasts, and firm, round buttocks, Nobue and the others crossed beyond admiration and lust to an overpowering sense of awe. They were aware of the desire to bow and scrape and lift their hands toward heaven like savages deifying a graven image. Yano actually scooted to one side, got down on his knees, and began to pray.

His prayer was in the form of a song—Nishida Sachiko's classic "After the Acacia Rain."

Like *Messiah* or *Requiem*, the song swelled to include the others' voices as well. The five of them lost all sense of time, muttering, "Whoa . . . whoa," in the intervals between lines of the lyric as they watched the woman with the unbelievable body dance. They had sung five choruses when the silhouette slid off the curtain and disappeared into some other part of the apartment— presumably the shower room. But the five maintained their prayerlike positions. In the space of about ten minutes, everyone had undergone a complete spiritual renewal.

"That was *awesome*," Kato said with a sigh when they'd returned to the table. "Hey, O-Sugi, have a beer," Nobue barked, and handed Sugiyama another can. Ishihara chomped hungrily into his croquettes but neglected to remove them from the packaging first. Styrofoam—or perhaps plastic wrap—got caught in his throat, and as his face turned blue he began laughing and spraying croquette crumbs. This long-awaited laughter from Ishihara sealed the collective mood-shift, and Yano tossed all three remaining salted beans in his mouth at once, clapped his hands, and shouted, "Everyone! May I have your attention, please!" He supervised an impromptu scraping-together of capital, and the party-as-usual began.

When Yano and Kato suddenly appeared at the top of the metal staircase on the old wood-frame, two-story apartment building and came clattering down, Henmi Midori, who'd just relieved Suzuki Midori on stakeout, tensed up. Thinking the enemy was on the move, she immediately pressed the SEND button on her mobile phone. Tomiyama Midori and Takeuchi Midori were already stationed near the deserted cove above Atami, but Suzuki Midori had parked her car at a family restaurant about a hundred meters up the street from Nobue's and was inside drinking a cappuccino. She had taken only three sips when her beeper went off. Her throat instantly went cotton-dry, but the cappuccino was still too hot to gulp down. Reminding herself that she mustn't let on to the other customers or the waitresses how nervous she was, she stood up and strolled woodenly toward the public phone near the entrance. In fact, no one was paying any attention to her whatsoever, but as she slowly approached the green telephone, she was internally rehearsing her role: *I'm a naughty suburban housewife, and I'm about to arrange a rendezvous with my secret lover. . . .*

"Hi, sweetie. It's me. Any news?"

Sorry. Looks like I jumped the gun.

"Oh . . . so you're still at the office?"

Yes. I thought everyone was leaving, but it was only a couple of them going on some sort of errand. I'm afraid I'm still stuck here.

"I'll be waiting, darling."

Suzuki Midori went back to her seat and thirstily swallowed half of the now-lukewarm cappuccino.

Henmi Midori had come to understand, over the past few weeks, just how difficult it is to perform surveillance on a building. Nothing looks more unnatural in contemporary suburban Tokyo than loitering on the street at night, no matter who you are or how you're dressed. She had given a great deal of thought as to how one could best blend into the scenery, however, and had shared her ideas in the study groups. Perhaps best of all would be to bring an infant or a small child or an elderly person with you. No one would be suspicious if you were with someone who required care and assistance—unless it was the middle of the night, maybe. But a dog was the perfect accessory at any time of day or night. Henmi Midori had once staked out Nobue's apartment in the company of a friend's Shih Tzu—an adorable, shaggy little thing. What with cleaning up after the Shih Tzu using the reversed plastic bag technique and having college girls stop to pet the beast and squeal "*Kawaii!*" she had begun almost to feel like an actual resident of the neighborhood. She often wore a jogging suit and carried a sports drink. Tonight she was dressed casually in sweater and sneakers and jeans, dangling a shopping bag, and keenly alive to the fact that the later it got, the more unnatural it looked for her to be there.

Yano and Kato returned bearing plastic bags from both the

convenience store and the liquor shop and bounded up the metal stairs. This neighborhood was right on the border between the shopping and residential districts. With the twenty-four-hour convenience store just down the street, people came and went at all hours, but after midnight, when the liquor shop and the video rental shop on either side of the convenience store closed, the street would grow dark and quiet. Once the last train on the Keio Line had gone, passersby would be few and far between.

About ten minutes before the video shop would close its shutters and call it a night, a drunk approached Henmi Midori and asked for directions. He had climbed unsteadily out of a taxi and shouted after it as it drove away—"Asshole!"—then staggered toward Henmi Midori and said, "Excuse me, is Block Two of Section Two around here?" She couldn't get a clear sense of the man's age from his face or clothing—he might have been considerably younger than herself, or considerably older—and she wondered anxiously if he wasn't a plainclothes policeman putting on a drunk act.

"I'm just waiting for a friend who lives in that apartment building there, so I'm afraid I don't know this area well, but, let's see. . . . I wonder if it isn't straight up this street? I know Block Six is over that way, and this is Block Seven—you see the sign on that telephone pole? So . . ."

That's right, that's exactly right, the man said in a defeated voice.

"I'm going back to my house. Not really a house, it's an apartment. I'm alone right now. Been alone for three months. Sachiko said the reason she was leaving was because I didn't get that post in Singapore, but sure enough it turns out she had another man. Some guy who lives a real flashy lifestyle, they tell me, drives a

Jaguar and everything, but, you know, about six months ago, this bottle of baby oil came tumbling out of her handbag, and I picked it up and said, 'What's this?' and she said she uses it to keep her skin from getting too dry, but I bet she was actually using it to do nasty things with this flashy man of hers. Exactly what kinds of nasty things, I couldn't tell you, but maybe rubbing it here and there, or using it to make things slide easier, and so forth. Er, forgive me. I already knew where Block Two was, but I asked you anyway because I wanted to have, you know, a normal conversation. Just a regular conversation. After the Singapore thing fell through, all Sachiko and I ever did was argue. And with women in bars it's just, 'Come on, let's go to a hotel!' 'No way!'—like that. I tried ordering in one of those, you know, erotic massages, but it was fifteen thousand yen an hour, so forget about normal conversation. But you, you very kindly tried to help, and I really appreciate that, I really really appreciate it. But, listen, I have a favor to ask you. . . ."

Even after he'd gone on and on like this, Henmi Midori still had no clue as to the man's age. It wasn't that it was too dark to see his face; it was just that there was nothing in his features or voice—or anything else about him—that suggested the energy of a living being. He was like a ghost drifting between death and birth, and you got the sense that if you reached out to touch his raincoat your hand might go right through him, as if he were made of thin air.

"Don't hurt anybody, okay?" the man said. "I don't mean me, I mean I hope you won't hurt *anyone*. It's not good to hurt people. Definitely not a good thing."

"I understand," Henmi Midori said, and the man said, "Thank you, thank you," any number of times as he staggered off. She watched him until he was well down the road and then muttered, "Idiot." *What do you know about being hurt?* she thought. *What about people who've been murdered?* Ever since the death of Iwata Midori, Henmi Midori had made a practice just before going to sleep or just after waking up, not of masturbating, as she had previously done every other day or so, but of pinching the flesh of her own cheeks or lips, hard. The bullet had made a fist-sized hole in Iwata Midori's face, and there wasn't much the mortician could do to fix that for the wake. The open casket had been horrible to behold. *Poor Wataa! It must have hurt so bad!* Even now, Henmi Midori's eyes would fill with tears each time this thought occurred to her. Just pinching your own face really hurt—what if a hot piece of lead chewed a big, ragged hole in it? What if something like that happened to a member of your family, right before your eyes? The mere thought was like a fire in Henmi Midori's inner workings. It nauseated her just trying to imagine how she would feel if her own father or mother or son or daughter had a hole blasted in their face or chest and died crying out in agony. She had always thought of people who did terrible things to other people as a completely different species of human being, but . . .

A lot of noise was now coming from the apartment she was watching. She could hear the dirtbags' laughter from here. It sounded as if they were playing rock-paper-scissors. Over the weeks of surveillance, Henmi Midori had come to know all their faces. Even putting aside what they'd done to Wataa, there was something repulsive and unpardonable about those faces. What sort of upbringing could have resulted in features like that? She often thought how good it would feel to slaughter them all, along with all their parents and brothers and sisters, in the cruelest way imaginable.

One of them came down the metal staircase, mumbling something under his breath. He got in the step van and started the engine. Henmi Midori pressed the SEND button on her phone again.

"Everyone's leaving the office, darling. Hurry up and come get me."

8

Love Me to the Bone

The rock-paper-scissors contest ended with Yano taking first place, followed by Kato, Sugiyama, Nobue, and Ishihara, in that order. Nobue and Ishihara loaded the costumes and equipment in the HiAce, and everyone climbed aboard. Ishihara drove. "I don't get it, I just don't get it," he kept muttering in a singsongy sort of way as he steered. He'd never, ever, come in dead last before, and therefore it was the first time he'd ever had to drive. The rock-paper-scissors competition wasn't a tournament but rather a showdown: all players at once. The contestants shouted, jumped up and down, laughed hysterically, rolled on the floor, knocked their heads against walls, went into spasms in every limb, and occasionally even vomited from overexcitement. The peculiar thing was that these frenetic performances actually seemed to affect the outcome. Things like statistical probabilities and psychic foresight were useless with a group like this; the deciding factor seemed to have more to do with concentration. Like the Yoruba or Herero or other warlike West African tribes performing rituals prior to battle, they would tense their entire bodies, jump about feverishly, bug out their eyes, and screech or roar at the top of their lungs, and for some reason the one who succeeded in most intimidating the others in this way always seemed to win. Ishihara was usually able to completely shred his opponents' jan-ken-pon rhythm. When the count began he would take on the aspect of a Tarahumara shaman with a belly-ful of peyote, or a cabaret hostess who's shot up too much speed, or a Siamese cat with hot pepper stuffed up its ass. No one was able to pierce his concentration barrier and force him to stick to the proper rhythm. Instead, they'd lose their own rhythm laughing nervously in response to his sudden, explosive, and utterly unhinged cackling. And yet tonight, for the first time ever, Ishihara had been defeated in round one. Not only was he forbidden to participate in the performance; he wasn't even permitted to drink. His job was simply to drive them to the location, help set up the lights and video cameras and sound system, wait soberly until the performance was over, and then drive them all back to Nobue's.

He knew it wasn't that he'd lacked his normal vigor tonight.

He'd led the others in the count while performing a series of so-called Erotic Calisthenics, which he claimed to have learned from an article in a sex rag and which involved pumping his limbs, twisting his body, and rolling his neck—simultaneously and at astonishing speeds—while laughing so explosively that it seemed as if the skin might peel off his face. At "pon" he threw down paper. Nobue too had paper—and both of them were eliminated, Yano and Sugiyama and Kato showing scissors. In the playoff with Nobue for last place, Ishihara changed tactics and performed a certain physical ceremony that he believed to be an esoteric form of yoga. While producing a dolphinish, ultra-high-frequency squeal from somewhere deep in his throat, he used both hands to scratch himself feverishly from crotch to scalp while shuffling his feet like Muhammad Ali—a tactic that usually resulted in his opponent suddenly deciding that there were more important things in life than rock-paper-scissors. Nobue, faced with Ishihara performing his ceremony and shrieking, "Not when I do YOGAYOGAYO-GAAAAAAAAAH!" had already admitted defeat to himself as he backed away and meekly held out scissors. Ishihara, scratching at his crotch and chest with his left hand, certain of victory and caterwauling his war cry, came up once again with paper. He stood there for some time, stunned and staring blankly at his open palm. Then he turned and trudged outside to warm up the van. His face was smiling, his eyes glittered in the late autumn moonlight, and he emitted a flickering aura that might have triggered seizures in an impartial but sensitive child, and yet he was strangely depressed. *I just don't get it*, he kept muttering.

By the time they reached Fuchu Avenue, the party was in full swing in the rear of the van. Kato, testing his sea legs in the swaying and rocking vehicle, was selecting the costumes for the evening. Yano, beside himself at having taken first place for the first time in some eight months, was smiling and babbling to himself.

"I can't believe it! To think that I—*I*—will sing lead vocal. . . . I haven't achieved anything like this since grade school, when I did an imitation of Tony Tani singing "Abacus Cha-cha-cha" at the school talent show, and they called me back for an encore, gave me a standing ovation and everything, and . . ."

Nobue tried to interrupt to ask Yano what song he wanted to sing tonight, but he couldn't get through, so Kato selected a song instead. "Yano-rin, Yano-rin, 'Love Me to the Bone' is okay with you, right?" Kato shook him by the shoulder, but Yano just smiled to himself and went on with the story no one else was listening to.

"The thing is, I was level one with the abacus, and there was this asshole in my class named Nakayama, and I challenged him with his electronic calculator, and I won, I beat him. But the thing about this Nakayama, when he was fourteen, for some reason, even though he wasn't sick or anything but I guess just because his hair was a little thin, he started wearing a toupee. I guess it was his parents' idea, but one time during an earthquake drill it slipped off and everybody found out he wore a rug, and he went ballistic, started hitting and kicking everybody. That's the sort of asshole he was, but of course the toupee incident was way after I beat his calculator with my abacus, but . . ." The story was of no interest whatsoever to anyone, but there seemed no indication that it would ever end.

Sugiyama had come in third, which meant he was one of the backup singers, so he was warming up his voice, going,

AAAAHHHHH, between slugs of booze, which he was urging upon the others as well. Yano and Kato had bought several two-liter aluminum "kegs" of beer and a large bottle of Suntory White whiskey at Goro-chan, the corner liquor shop, and they were shunting the bottle and kegs around as if they were rugby balls. In short order they were all shitfaced. Kato selected, from the nearly twenty costumes they'd pooled their money to buy, a suit of the sort worn by *enka* singers in cheesy cabarets—blue satin with faux-gold-foil lapels, a matching shirt, and a "butterfly" bow tie. He changed into the suit, though doing so while drunk in a moving vehicle was bound to cause the nausea of which he promptly and cheerfully complained. When he was finished dressing himself he undressed Yano, even as the latter obliviously continued his tale of the abacus, and then, as if changing the clothes on a mannequin or a Barbie doll, poured him into a leather bondage suit criss-crossed with zippers. The bottom of the leather suit was a miniskirt, and the straps on top had two metallic red roses attached at nipple level. It fit the emaciated Yano like a dream, and Sugiyama and Kato lifted their voices in a raucous cheer that was visible as a fine, beery mist. The abacus tale rolled on even as Kato slicked back Yano's hair, applied lipstick to his lips, and packed him into black fishnet stockings and high heels. Sugiyama, meanwhile, was rehearsing the night's song in a sequined rayon kimono, but he had tied the obi too tight and suddenly regurgitated. Yano slipped on the vomit in his high heels and fell to the floor as Sugiyama, never missing a beat, belted out the final words to "Love me to the Bone" and then shouted for Ishihara to play the tape again. As they entered the Tomei Expressway, Ishihara was singing along with the others but, partially because he hadn't had any alcohol since leaving Nobue's apartment, he just couldn't shake an odd, nagging feeling that something was wrong. By the time they reached the Odawara-Atsugi Road, the usual chaos and confusion in the rear of the van had attained new levels of dementia, and even the normally rather calm and collected Kato was standing with his head out the side window, fluids oozing from his eyes and nose and ears as he sang, between spasms of projectile vomiting: "To the bone, to the bone, want you to love me to the bone!"

Watching Yano and Sugiyama and Kato guzzling the beer and whiskey and singing refrain after refrain, Nobue couldn't help but smile. The three of them, usually relatively subdued, were in incredibly high spirits tonight. There was vomit all over the floor of the van, yes, but—hell, at least they were having fun. Savoring the cold air coming in through the window, Nobue decided to have a smoke and climbed into the passenger seat next to Ishihara.

"What's the matter, Ishi-kun?" he asked as he lit his cigarette. "I mean, I know you lost at rock-paper-scissors and everything, but I've never seen you so quiet. Anything wrong?"

Ishihara's eyes were extravagantly bloodshot. Unaccustomed to driving, he always kept his eyes open as wide as they would go when behind the wheel.

"Kato and Yano and Sugiyama are totally out of their minds," Nobue went on, rolling down the passenger-side window. "There's hardly any whiskey or beer left back there. It's, like, the first time those three have ever really let go like this."

"Nobu-chin," Ishihara said, his eyes still protruding abnormally. "I don't know. I've got a bad feeling about this. . . ."

...

Ishihara parked at their spot by the seashore, some ten kilometers short of Atami. It was down a narrow, inconspicuous road that branched off from the Manazuru Highway and ended at an enormous concrete breakwater. Yano and Kato and Sugiyama had piled drunkenly out of the van and were standing unsteadily on the beach with microphones in their fists, shouting "Hurry up!" while Ishihara and Nobue struggled with the karaoke machine, lights, and video cameras. Nobue switched on the van's interior lamp to give Ishihara some light to work by, then ran out to the beach. None of them noticed the four middle-aged women hiding behind a gigantic concrete tetrapod a mere twenty meters away.

The small beach lay in a horseshoe cove beyond the curving concrete breakwater. The breakwater was about three meters high, and the narrow, winding road that led to it was bordered on either side by thick groves of pine and other trees. No one would be able to see them from the road or from up or down the coast, even after they'd turned on the lights. Only from the sea could they have been spotted, but few fishing boats are out late on Saturday nights in Atami Bay. Nor was this cove the sort of place any tourists or locals would ever visit for sightseeing or romantic walks. The random jumble of giant concrete

wave-dissipating tetrapods, like mutant versions of children's
jacks, marred the scenery; an ambient smell of sewage hung
over the beach, which was approximately the size of a basketball
court and consisted more of rocks than sand; and rusted jum-
bles of steel—the discarded engines of fishing boats, perhaps, or
trucks—added a cold, metallic vibe to the already desolate and
forbidding atmosphere.

Some two years earlier, Yano, finding himself with absolutely
nothing to do on a Sunday afternoon, had sat in his apartment
listening over and over again to a recording of house-style noise
music until he became convinced that he was literally on the
verge of losing his mind. Hoping to avoid a psychotic break, he'd
called on Kato and dragged him out for a long bus journey that
involved any number of transfers and ended at the seashore,
along which they were walking silently when they'd stumbled
upon this cove. It didn't occur to them at the time that it might
be a good place for Karaoke Blasts (this being before the advent
of the ritual), but Kato discovered at one end of the beach a pair
of discarded, blood-drenched panties and later reported this
discovery to Nobue. Things had progressed from there. "The
penetrator always returns to the scene of the crime," Nobue had
declared, and each Saturday for the next ten weeks the entire
group had come here to stake out this beach. On the tenth trip,
Yano had said, "It might not've been a virgin getting her cherry
popped, you know. There's no proof that those panties didn't
belong to some fifty-year-old Oba-san who forgot her tampons,
right?" No sooner had this seed of doubt been vocalized than
everyone awoke as if from a dream. They suddenly saw that it
was perhaps overly optimistic to conclude from no more evidence than a single pair of muddy, bloodstained panties that

they would soon be in a position to witness the rape of an angelic but ultimately lascivious nymphet of the sort who populate adult videos. Nonetheless, it seemed a waste to abandon this spot they'd visited each week for two and a half months, so Ishihara had proposed that the cove be designated their permanent multipurpose special event space, and so it had remained ever since.

In the past, the winners of the top four places in the rock-paper-scissors showdown had always been granted the right to sing, but since Sugioka's death that number had been reduced to three. The division of responsibilities was clearly defined, and staff and cast never changed places in the course of a given night. Ishihara would therefore be stuck inside the van, along with the noisy portable generator, which was strapped down in the rear to keep the racket it made from interfering with the performances. Two cords extended from the generator through a narrow opening in the window and out to the beach, where they were connected to two video cameras, one secured to a tripod for the master shot of everyone on stage and one handheld by Nobue, who was to move around taking close-ups of each singer. The cameras were portable Sony 3CCD VX1s, the microphones cordless Sennheiser SY3s, and the speakers BOSE 501s. There was also a portable DAT deck and a simple mixing board in the van, the operation of which was up to Ishihara.

"Ishi-kun, please hurry!" Yano was shivering in his skimpy bondage gear. "Luckily I'm drunk, but it's fuckin' *cold* in this costume!" The three singers were facing the sea, waving their dead mikes impatiently and muttering, *One, two, one, two! Test, test!* Unfortunately, Ishihara had always been hopeless with mechanisms of any sort. In middle school, when the Walkman

first came out, a classmate of his had tricked him into insert-
ing the earbuds in his nostrils. It wasn't a big surprise that he
couldn't get the sound working now.

"If we wait for Ishihara to get it right, we'll be here till dawn,"
Sugiyama whined.

"All right, all right," said Nobue. "I'll go see what's holding
him up." He set the camera on the tetrapod behind the three
singers and headed back to the HiAce.

"*I* wish they'd gather together in one group," said Suzuki Midori.
The rocket launcher rested on her shoulder.

"One of them always stays in the van, to play engineer,"
Henmi Midori said, peering through her Zeiss binoculars,

All four Midoris were repulsed by the costumes. *Is this what
Japan struggled through its whole postwar history to achieve?*
Takeuchi Midori was asking herself. *Grown men in their mid-
twenties, dressed like perverts, whooping and cackling like morons
and singing karaoke out in the middle of nowhere?* The thought
literally nauseated her. *In this lonesome place, with the smell of
sewage and oil spill and rotten fish all around, wearing things not
even the tackiest provincial comedian would put on. . . . Especially
that little skinny one in the middle—what's with the leather miniskirt, for heaven's sake? And the one with the glasses and sequined
kimono, drinking beer straight from a two-liter keg and howling—
what would his mother say if she could see this?*

The moon cast a rippling silver ribbon over the surface of
the sea.

The Midoris were wearing ski gloves to prevent their hands

from getting too cold to operate the rocket launcher properly. They all had their hair tied back and wore black woolen ski masks that hid their faces, long-sleeved shirts and black sweaters under black waterproof windbreakers, and black trousers and hiking boots. Their breath made little white clouds, and they were all crouching down, breathing into their gloves so as not to give themselves away.

The speakers came on with a buzzing growl, and an amplified voice said: "Okay . . . okay, okay."

"Well, here goes." Suzuki Midori took off her gloves and, just as Sakaguchi had taught her and as she had subsequently practiced tens if not hundreds of times, opened the rear cover on the M72-A2 LAW, removed the carrying sling, and extended the inner tube.

"Don't forget," Henmi Midori whispered, "you have to aim at the tetrapod behind them. If you hit one of them directly, it won't work."

"I *know*," said Suzuki Midori, pursing her lips and focusing all her concentration on the front sight. She aimed at the tetrapod just behind the three sleazeballs in their demented outfits. The others crouched on either side of her to avoid the backblast, and Henmi Midori and Takeuchi Midori helped support the extended inner tube.

"Oh, God . . . I'm getting wet," murmured Tomiyama Midori.

Suzuki Midori hissed at her to snap out of it. "You've got your knife ready, right? Be prepared to use it on any survivors."

Just as the intro to "Love Me to the Bone" started up, with its vulgar tenor sax, Suzuki Midori unlocked the safety and pushed the trigger.

Six fins sprang out from the rear of the sixty-six-millimeter

HEAT rocket as it departed, and you could clearly see the warhead spinning as it zoomed toward the tetrapod. The backblast illuminated the air behind the Midoris with a brilliant ashen glow. Hearing the strange but deeply resonant *pa-SHOOP* sound and noticing the burst of light, the three dirtbags stopped singing and turned to look. In the next instant the warhead contacted the tetrapod and exploded with a deafening blast and an enormous ball of orange fire.

What the hell is that? Yano wondered as the spinning warhead traced a smoking arc toward them. He was thinking it looked like a rocket ship in some old movie with crappy special effects, when he found himself enveloped in blinding light and earsplitting sound. He was slammed to the rocky beach like a wet rag doll. Sugiyama was looking up at the video camera Nobue had left on the tetrapod when the explosion blew it to bits, and he opened his mouth to say *Whoa!* but of course had no time to do so. The rayon of his kimono burst into crackling flames, along with the sequins, as he lifted some two meters off the ground. Kato's first thought was that Nobue and Ishihara had prepared a special fireworks display. It was typical of Ishihara to overdo it like this, he thought, and he was about to start laughing when a fist-sized chunk of concrete from the tetrapod came along at a hundred meters per second and shaved off his lower jaw—flesh, bones, teeth, and all—even as he too began an ascent that would peak at an impressive three meters. The end result was a trio of disarticulated bodies that looked as if sharks had been snacking on them, with jagged chunks ripped from their arms and stomachs and necks—to say nothing of the fragments of tetrapod embedded in various parts of their flesh. In the twinkling of an eye their bodies had come to resemble bloody rags—rather like the discarded panties they'd once found on this very beach. All three of them were dead, of course.

At the moment of the explosion, Nobue had been stepping out of the HiAce to return to the beach and Ishihara had been in the rear, fiddling with the dials on the mixing console. The blast caused the entire van to shake and teeter, and both of them were knocked off their feet. Nobue face-planted on the ground outside, and Ishihara's head slammed against a corner of the generator. But the HiAce remained upright and more or less intact, and it had shielded them from the blast and the tetrapod fragments. Blood was gushing from a gash in Ishihara's forehead and flowing down his face, however, and this threw him into a panic. In reaction to the intense burst of light and the overpowering noise, his brain was frantically spinning its wheels, and he was about to try forcing an idiotic laugh in a bid to gain a grip, when Nobue jumped back inside the battered van and shouted:

"They're coming after us with knives!"

"What's 'knives'?" Ishihara asked. He was staring at a palmful of blood he'd collected from the miniature geyser at the top right corner of his forehead. "You mean knives like with blades?" Though unable to grasp what was happening, he was terrified in his own way. He'd never had blood squirt from his head before. Worried that it might prove fatal, he was desperately trying to push the blood back inside.

"Drive, dammit!" Nobue shouted. "They're coming this way! With knives! It's fuckin' crazy! Yano-rin and O-Sugi and Kato-kichi are dead! They're all in pieces!"

Ishihara looked at him uncomprehendingly, pressing his blood-soaked palm against the gash in his head. "Where's 'pieces'?" he asked, then added, "It's strange, you know—all this blood coming out but it doesn't even hurt. Why do you think that is, Nobu-chin? I mean, if you just cut the tip of your finger a little it hurts so bad you could scream, so how come this doesn't?"

It didn't look as if Ishihara would be doing any driving. Nobue spun toward the driver's seat, but as he did so he saw through the windshield the four masked, knife-wielding figures, who were now within a few steps of the van. He dived for the switches and locked all the doors. The four black-attired attackers, their faces hidden behind woolen ski masks, reached the van just as the locks clicked shut, and in an animalistic sort of frenzy they began pounding on the vehicle and rocking it back and forth. The explosion had blown out all the lights, and it was pitch-dark around the HiAce, but the dim interior lamp was just enough for Nobue to make out the figures outside. When all four of them raised the knives in their fists, Nobue too succumbed to panic, and urine soaked his boxer shorts as he plopped into the driver's seat. Ishihara was on the bench in the rear, still trying to push blood back inside his head. The driver's-side window was cracked where fragments of concrete had hit it, and two of the shadowy figures outside picked up baseball-sized rocks and began pounding them against the glass.

The window didn't break, however. Such was their frenzied state that Takeuchi Midori and Henmi Midori weren't even aware that all strength had drained from their arms. Nobue, meanwhile, was trying to turn an ignition key that wasn't there. His thumb and forefinger pressed against the ignition, gripping the nonexistent key and twisting clockwise and back, clockwise and back. He even tried going, *Vrooom, vrooom,* with his voice, but this of course had no effect either. "What's wrong with this thing?" he was muttering when, outside, Suzuki Midori shouted, "Gangway!" and slammed a rock the size of a baby's head against the side window. The glass folded in with a strange, fingernails-on-chalkboard sort of sound, which caused Ishihara finally to remove his hand from his head and look up. His face was smeared with blood on one side and completely drained of color on the other.

"Did you just hear like a super ultra mega-creepy sound, like somebody grinding their teeth?" he asked Nobue, who was still trying to start the van with the nonexistent key.

About a quarter of the window glass had given way, but now Suzuki Midori hesitated, unsure of what to do next. Surely if she had been thinking clearly she would either have (*a*) thrust her knife through the available opening or (*b*) knocked out the rest of the glass, unlocked the door, and forced her way inside. Neither of these alternatives occurred to her in the heat of the moment, however. The SDF man, Sakaguchi, hadn't shared any details on how to mop up survivors after a firefight. She knew she had memorized such sections in Green Beret manuals and guerrilla handbooks, but what with the roar and the blinding light of the explosion, the acrid smell of gunpowder, and the spectacle of three living bodies being literally blown apart, her brain seemed on fire and suddenly empty of any information whatsoever, including her own name and where she was and what she was doing. The other Midoris, whose ski-mask mouths resembled those of inflatable dolls, were trembling violently as they urged her on: "Stab them! Kill them all!"

"What're you doing, Nobu-chin?" said Ishihara. He was standing behind Nobue now, nudging his shoulder. "How can you start the engine when I've got the key?" Nobue didn't respond but continued to gape wide-eyed at the four attackers outside the windshield and side window. "Hey," Ishihara said, looking up, "there's some strange people out there wearing masks and— EEEK!—they've got knives!"

Suzuki Midori slammed the big rock against the window once more. A shower of bursting glass sprayed over Nobue, eliciting splotches of color on his pallid face, and the rock landed in his lap.

"Ishi-kun!" he screeched.

"Yes?" Ishihara replied, as if reading from a script.

"Help! They're trying to kill us!"

The Midoris, standing just outside the windowless door, heard him say this, of course. They were so close to Nobue that they could have stood on their tiptoes, leaned forward, and kissed him. Takeuchi Midori was shouting, "Suzuu, hurry up and open the door! Open the door!"

"What the fuck?" said Nobue, scooting away from them. "Ishi-kun, they're women! Oba-sans!"

As he tried to scramble over the seat to join Ishihara in the rear of the van, shards of glass rained from his clothing. A gloved hand reached through the window and lifted the lock button, and Suzuki Midori wrenched the door open and climbed aboard, awkwardly thrusting at Nobue with her Randall knife—a lagniappe Sakaguchi had thrown in with the rocket launcher. It was an unstudied move, but the weight of her body was behind it as she clambered aboard, and the tip of the blade was just at the right elevation to sink into the flesh of Nobue's cheek and slice through his gums, stopping only when it came into contact with the teeth on the other side. Nobue looked for a moment as if he didn't understand what had just happened, then tried to scream but found that the hardware inhibited his ability to produce any sounds. The other three Midoris screamed in his stead when they saw Suzuki Midori's blade buried in the enemy's cheek. It was this close-up view of a knife lodged in a face that finally drained the frenzy out of them. Henmi Midori felt something hot drip down the inside of her thigh and wondered if her period had begun unexpectedly, but of course it was only urine.

Tears had immediately formed in Nobue's eyes and were now streaming down his face. "It hurth!" he said, but moving his mouth made the blade twist and only intensified the pain. Suzuki Midori stood frozen for some moments after stabbing him. She felt as if she'd turned to stone, and her mind was still a complete blank—a state she'd never experienced before. The hand gripping the knife handle was trembling; so, in fact, was her entire arm. Time seemed to have come to a standstill, and no one knew what to do next, until Ishihara shuffled forward, reached out, and lifted the ski mask covering her face. She let out a startled, "Kyaah!"

"You're right, it really is a woman," Ishihara said, and then, as if to release all his tension and fear, he began laughing the most powerful, eldritch, and supernatural laugh he'd ever produced.

It was like an exorcistic incantation recorded and played back at high speed and earsplitting volume, and it vibrated in one's brain and burrowed into one's stomach and seemed capable of causing the air and all living beings along the entire seacoast to freeze solid and then quickly decompose. In the short intervals between bursts of laughter, Ishihara tossed out words whose meaning wasn't clear—*woman, Oba-san, pig, hullabaloo, jerk-off, sex, I love you,* and so forth—and Suzuki Midori, suddenly seized with unspeakable fear, began puking. Trying to cover her mouth, she let go of the knife, which then fell out of Nobue's cheek and clattered heavily to the floor. The other Midoris rushed to support the sagging and still-regurgitating Suzuki and began their retreat, dragging her along with them. Ishihara pressed his handkerchief against Nobue's cheek and, chuckling, took the ignition key from his own pocket.

Retreating across the beach, the Midoris had no choice but to view once again what remained of Yano and Kato and Sugiyama. They didn't want to see but couldn't avoid looking down, as they had to watch their steps in the darkness. Sugiyama's stomach was ripped open vertically, and his intestines were hanging out, looking exactly like the *dae-chang* Henmi Midori had once eaten at a Korean barbecue place, and she too vomited. One of Yano's eyes had melted and was oozing out of its socket, and the lower half of Kato's face was missing, so that his head resembled a grotesque but marvelously realistic half mask. Takeuchi Midori, seeing someone's hand lying all by itself at her feet, noted its resemblance to a starfish and began to weep. Crabs and sea lice were already feasting on Yano's melted eye, and when Tomiyama

Midori happened to catch a glimpse of this, she screamed and then doubled over, holding her stomach and heaving. The four Midoris were still moaning and retching when they finally reached the car, and all of them were thinking something along the same lines: *That's it. No more. That's enough revenge.*

9

Dreams Anytime

The four Midoris disbanded the Midori Society and decided not to meet or even to contact one another for the time being. The rocket attack at the seashore just above Atami was treated as big news in the media. The authorities were investigating it as the probable work of some extremist political faction, and the four Midoris avoided all suspicion. Their names never even came up in the investigation. For one thing, the Midori Society wasn't on anyone's list of dangerous groups—left-wing terrorists, right-wing fanatics, organized crime syndicates, motorcycle gangs, and what have you. Local law enforcement enlisted the help of the National Police Agency, and the forensic analysis upon which Japan prides itself was brought into full play but got no further than identifying the weapon as a portable rocket launcher. The authorities had no idea how anyone could have gotten their hands on such a weapon. The Self-Defense Forces publicly announced that M72s were not among the weapons in their arsenal, and off the record they cast suspicion on American forces in Japan. The American military, for their part, took the attitude that it wasn't their problem if a nation of dim-witted peaceniks wanted to make such a fuss over something that amounted to a virtual nonevent when compared to, say, the Los Angeles riots—which attitude was vehemently criticized in *Asahi Shimbun* editorials.

Nonetheless, had Ishihara been an average human being, or Nobue a normal one, the four members of the Midori Society might very well have been called in for questioning. Ishihara had gotten a look at Suzuki Midori's face, and it's possible that if he had said, *I saw one of the killers. It was an Oba-san*, the investigating officers might have thought of connecting the incident to the murder of Iwata Midori, the woman who'd been shot with a Tokarev. But it wasn't as if Ishihara were holding anything back out of concern about the investigation widening to include the Tokarev incident. Both he and Nobue were called in to talk with the police several times, but the investigators couldn't make sense of anything they said. The noun "Oba-san" did issue from Ishihara's mouth from time to time, but always seemingly at random, in the midst of a confused and disconnected ramble, so that it never piqued the investigators' interest.

"Nobu-chin took a knife in the cheek and I lost at

rock-paper-scissors but before that the girl in the apartment across the way got bare-ass naked—Gyah ha ha ha! I mean *bare-ass*! *Suppon-pon*! Turtle soup's on! What? BARE ASS me again! Ha ha!—and I couldn't concentrate on the rock-paper-scissors, so I lost, I went with paper and lost and it made me so mad I thought about peeing all over the karaoke set and speakers but I didn't have to pee and nothing came out but I was thinking, you know, when Nobu-chin got stabbed with the knife it was so intense, it reminded me of when they cut a wedding cake, and I thought about singing the wedding song, like *dan danka dan!* but I couldn't remember the melody and nothing came out but instead it was like on *The Bold Shogun* where there's this villain who always wears a mask but when they unmask him he turns out to be an Oba-san, and the Oba-san goes, like, 'What *are* you insinuating?' but the truth is she's really evil and I always end up watching it because it's on right after *Sailor Moon*, but not really like wedding cake but more like when one of the villain's thugs skewers like a weak little kid with his sword and it goes *pu-shutt*, that's what it reminded me of, I mean, it was really funny and everything, but then . . ."

Ishihara was sent for a psychological evaluation and diagnosed as suffering from either schizophrenia or advanced and probably untreatable mania. The investigators had no choice but to give up on trying to get information from him. As for Nobue, since the knife had pierced his cheek, sliced through his gums, and shredded his tongue, he was unable to speak intelligibly even after leaving the hospital and gave the appearance of being severely mentally challenged. Eventually the police formed an unspoken consensus that murdering such unsalvageable youths was probably a service to the nation anyway, and the mass media, for its part, gradually moved on to other sensational stories. The real wall that the investigation had run up against, however, was the lack of any discernible chain of events. Crimes that don't have any clear motive are the most difficult to solve, and tying a rocket attack at the beach to three random murders in Chofu was a leap far beyond the imaginative powers of the police. The investigators briefly pursued the theory that the attack might have been perpetrated by a tribe of local juvenile delinquents angered by the late-night karaoke sessions, or by a roving motorcycle gang that claimed the roads in that region as their own territory, but after some five months with no concrete results the investigation was terminated.

By that time, the four Midoris had let down their guard somewhat and begun communicating occasionally by telephone, although they still forbade any meetings in person. Strangely, all four of them were leading much more fulfilling lives than ever before and exuding newfound self-assurance. One of the Midoris became the most popular person in her workplace, and another was employee of the week seven weeks in a row. A third found that communication with her son had improved dramatically: he now opened up to her about his feelings and interests, his performance at school was improving, and he no longer spent hours at a time silently playing computer games. And the fourth Midori fell in love with a much younger man she'd met at a karaoke club. *You have this serenity about you . . . that's so soothing to the heart . . . and at the same time . . . this vibrant, electric tension. . . . How do you do it?* Such were the things the handsome, aquiline-nosed twenty-six-year-old graduate of Kyoto University, who was employed by a think tank for a major brokerage firm, would whisper to the mid-thirties Midori as he treated her to passionate and tender cunnilingus. What all four Midoris shared was an indelible, very serious, and very real secret—a secret that served both to bolster their self-confidence and to lend them a certain air of mystery. And that combination of self-possession and intrigue is what makes a woman truly appealing, especially when she herself seems unaware of it.

Outwardly, the Midoris' daily lives differed in no significant way from those of their coworkers and neighbors. But the three shredded corpses, the knife in Nobue's cheek, and Ishihara's more-powerful-than-a-rocket-launcher laughter were not the sorts of things one simply dismisses from one's mind. It was surprising how many things in this world could remind one of coils of intestines protruding from a ruptured stomach, or thirty centimeters of blackened, mangled tongue hanging from a ruined mouth, or a burned and detached, starfishlike hand. Organs and body parts that had been separated from their parent bodies and lost all purpose or function did not really resemble anything else in this world, and precisely for that reason almost any unusual sight or smell was enough to trigger those memories. Normally, for people who've witnessed such horrors—soldiers returning from foreign wars, for example—flashbacks of this sort are often harbingers of severe post-traumatic stress disorders. Even a single experience of something as unimaginably gruesome as what they'd witnessed can cause PTSD, and there have been countless reports of people developing such disorders after seeing friends or relatives die before their eyes in traffic accidents, fires, or natural disasters. But for the Midoris, who possessed a blind and unshakable belief in their own righteousness, the memories had the opposite effect. The battle at Atami had been a kind of holy war for them—they were, after all, avenging the murders of valued friends—and as such it was not something they felt any need to be ashamed of. The experience had, in fact, boosted their self-esteem, and they seemed to ooze fulfillment from every pore. They were, nonetheless, of the gentler sex and not without maternal instincts. The recurring image of those mangled corpses naturally helped to dampen their exhilaration and to prevent their becoming overly intoxicated with themselves. And so they lived with their real-life nightmare, neither glorifying nor denying it. In any case, they had emerged victorious.

If it wasn't for this guy right here, Nobue was thinking as he gazed at Ishihara, *I would have lost my mind long ago.* They were in Nobue's apartment, some seven months after the incident at Atami. The wound in Nobue's cheek had healed over, but he was still recovering and haunted by the trauma he had suffered that night. His tongue was mutilated, his scarred cheek pinched and tended to twitch, and he still couldn't speak normally. He had quit his part-time job in computer sales, but he wasn't in particularly straitened circumstances. His parents, in response to their son's misfortune at having been maimed in a senseless but spectacular attack that had been big news in all the national media, faithfully sent him a regular and rather considerable allowance. As for Ishihara, how he managed to pull it off is anyone's guess, but since the attack he had continued to commute each weekday to his job at a small design firm. And when Saturday came around, he was sure to show up at Nobue's apartment, calling, *No-o-bu-u–chi-i-n!* as he climbed the stairs outside. In short, there was essentially no change in him whatsoever.

At the moment, Ishihara was nudging Nobue's shoulder and

saying, "Nobu-chin! Nobu-chin, say 'Congratulations on the New Year'!" The closest Nobue could get was something like, *Kon raw yoo rayon la la Roo Ya*, at which Ishihara collapsed on the tatami and rolled about, laughing hysterically. Nobue didn't mind. He knew now that when you've been badly damaged emotionally or physically, it isn't the people who are mournfully sympathetic or overly careful about your feelings that help you out so much as those who treat you as they've always done. "GYAAAAAH!" Now Ishihara was on his feet again, nudging Nobue's shoulder and bouncing up and down. "Nobu-chin, please, I'm begging you, now say, 'Red pussy blue pussy yellow pussy.' Please please please. I swear I won't laugh." As Nobue gazed at his old friend, a tear of gratitude rolled down his cheek. All at once he realized how much he loved this person, and he grabbed the hand nudging his shoulder and clasped it tightly in his own. "Thank you, Ishi-kun," he said hoarsely. Ishihara was so startled by both the gesture and the sentiment that he wondered if his friend had finally broken under the strain and gone mental. He pressed his forehead against Nobue's to see if the poor lad wasn't running a fever.

They would need a little more time before they'd be ready to rise to the final battle.

More than half a year went by. There had been no Saturday Karaoke Blasts in all that time, of course, since the troupe of six had been diminished by four. Nobue's rehabilitation continued. On a sunny afternoon in late fall, he and Ishihara were strolling along shoulder to shoulder and all but hand in hand beside Koshu Avenue in Chofu. They were like the last two specimens, both male, of a soon-to-be-extinct species, exploring their narrow game preserve. Now that his cheek wound had healed to a permanent scar, Nobue in particular felt as if he'd aged tremendously. They were passing the Koganei Electronics Institute when he said, with only a barely noticeable speech defect, "There was a guy named Sugioka once, wasn't there?" Ishihara was carrying a Garigari-Kun popsicle in each hand, licking now one, now the other, and chanting things like, "Popsicles for autumn, popsicles in autumn, two popsicles on a warm autumn day! Two skinny weenies getting sucked, sucked off! The first one to squirt's gonna win first prize!" But at the mention of Sugioka's name he stopped. "Nobu-chin, what sort of a guy was Sugioka again?" he asked, and began to skip in a circle. It was, by any measure, a strange sight—a small man in his mid-twenties with a remarkably large head and eyes, sucking alternately on two popsicles and skipping in circles around another man of about the same age with equally oversized peepers, a nasty scar on his cheek, and a prematurely receding hairline. Other pedestrians on the street would catch a glimpse of Ishihara and quickly lower their gaze to avoid any sort of eye contact or interaction as they passed. "Quit dancing around me like a crazy Indian," Nobue kept saying, though in fact he was enjoying the silliness. Finally Ishihara skipped to a halt and squatted abruptly on the pavement, holding his head and complaining of dizziness. Then he bounced up again. "Garigari-Kun A," he said to the bare popsicle stick in his right hand, "may you rest in peace. Garigari-Kun B, now it's your turn to die!" After chomping down on what remained of the second popsicle, he turned to Nobue and said, "Seriously, I can't remember—what was Sugioka like? I seem to recall that he was skinny and had a narrow face and loved knives and mumbled a lot and you couldn't tell if he was gloomy or cheerful, but there's lots of guys like that. I wish I could picture him clearly, like in a flashback in a movie or somethin', but I can't."

Nobue responded with a suggestion.

"Why don't we go look at the place where he was killed? It's not far from here."

On a late November afternoon like this, when the weather was fine and the sunshine warm on your shoulders, any normal person would be outside if possible, so naturally the junior college girl was in her room. Spying Nobue and Ishihara out her window, she opened it to lean out and call to them, "Hi! What a surprise!" Nobue, on hearing that voice and looking up to see that face protruding from the window, felt as if the wound on his cheek had been reopened and his tongue resliced. Ishihara let out a terrified, "GYAH!" and buckled at the knees. "Run!" they whispered to each other, but the junior college girl said, "Wait there! I happen to be free just now! I'll be down in a sec!" and a moment later they heard the rapid *dan dan dan dan dan* of her steps on the wooden stairs. Nobue and Ishihara were in a state resembling sleep paralysis as their brains tried to process the afterimage of the junior college girl's face. Unable to move, they were still shivering at the image when the actual face materialized before them, seeming to cause the blue sky to crack in two and the yellow ginkgo leaves to turn to scraps of rotting flesh, fluttering in the breeze. Both of them felt as if they'd just slurped up their own vomit.

"Long time no see! Did you come to visit your friend again?" the junior college girl said, twisting her already asymmetrical face even further out of line with what was probably meant to be a smile. What a relief it would be, Nobue and Ishihara were thinking, if only the skin of that face would just go ahead and peel back to reveal a reptilian alien or a beast of the underworld or something. Their legs felt as if rooted to the ground.

"For boys with such funny faces, you sure are loyal to your friends!"

Nobue wondered what sort of face he had, if the owner of one such as this thought it funny. An image flashed through his mind of Hundred Eyes, the ghostly goblin from *Ge Ge Ge no Kitaro*, and he had the sickening sensation that he had been transformed into some such goblin or ghost. Without thinking he raised two limp wrists and moaned, "Mark me . . ." There was nothing funny about this, but the junior college girl cried, "Stop it!" and put both hands over her mouth, giggling exactly like the protagonist of a girls' manga: *Ku ku ku ku ku ku!* Ishihara felt as if his entire brain had broken out in a bumpy rash. Instinctively sensing that he must act or risk a sudden descent into madness, he hollered a meaningless, "Yo-de-lady-who!"

"You two are so funny!" the junior college girl said, and giggled again, and it seemed as if the nightmare might repeat itself endlessly. "That friend of yours . . ." she said. "What was his name again?"

Nobue felt as if he were going to pee his pants. "Su . . . Sugi-oka," he said, unwisely lifting his eyes. This gave him a close-up of the junior college girl's face, and he actually did leak a few drops.

"Oh, that's right, Sugioka-kun. He still comes here a lot, you know. He just stands there crying and crying."

Ishihara let out a shriek and sank to his haunches, and hot tears filled Nobue's eyes. The tears were not for Sugioka, of course, but simply a product of abject terror.

"Sometimes, when conditions are right, I see things like that. Like in my room in the dormitory here, now and then I see this girl in her early teens standing by the bookcase, and then one time I noticed that her feet kept disappearing, and it dawned on me that she was a ghost, because the ghosts in stories always don't have feet, and that explained a lot. Sometimes I see them at the pool too, but . . ."

No! Ishihara and Nobue inwardly cried out. *Please don't take a face like that to a swimming pool!* But paralysis prevented them from displaying any emotion.

"I see mostly little kids there, floating in the water with their hair all spread out and wavy. It happens a lot when my body's exhausted or my nerves are frayed."

Tired, are you? Then why don't you go lie down somewhere for, like, FOREVER? Try the Elephants' Graveyard!

"I always see Sugioka-kun standing right over there with a big open gash in his neck, and it looks like all the blood has drained out of him, because he's about twice as skinny as when he was alive and used to pee there all the time, but I feel sorry for him because he just stands there and looks frustrated and cries. He says he can't go anywhere else, he's afraid to, and no one comes to help him. 'All I can do is stand here and cry,' he says, 'but nobody notices me, and it was always my dream to go jogging with a pretty girl but now I don't have any feet so I'll never be able to do that, and my friends are all being murdered, getting blown to pieces and dying with their guts spilling from their stomachs and their eyeballs hanging out, and all I can do is stand here and cry, and it's boring and lonely but now it's too late to change anything,' he says."

The two of them slogged back to Nobue's apartment, unable even to speak as they suppressed simultaneous urges to urinate, defecate, and regurgitate and battled dizziness, palpitations, and chills. The junior college girl's face and voice, and her figure and words and body odor, had drained them of every last scintilla of energy, and both of them were reliving all the unfortunate turns of events and traumas and physical and emotional wounds and maledictions and enmities and jealousies they'd ever experienced. Under the terrible weight of these various evils they collapsed just inside the door and slumped there, incapable even of raising their heads.

"Wa-water . . . somebody give me water," Nobue said, but Ishihara couldn't move, and though he made an effort to laugh several times he couldn't get the muscles of his mouth and cheeks to budge either. Suddenly realizing that he'd forgotten what laughter was, he wondered if this might be the end, if this was how he was going to die.

Eventually the sunny late autumn afternoon drew to a close. As the room sank into darkness, Nobue began to weep. Between convulsive sobs, he spat out the words, "Fucking hell!" Ishihara picked up on the rhythm and tried to imitate it. Hic, hic, hic. Fucking hell! *What is that rhythm?* he wondered. *It's like reggae.* Hic, hic, hic, hic. Fucking hell! Hic, hic. Through the window

on the far side of the darkened room they saw a light go on in
the apartment across the parking lot. Maybe one of these nights
they'd see the woman with the unbelievable body dancing in
nude silhouette again, they were both thinking even as they continued their *Fucking hell!* duet. After repeating bar after bar of
the sobbing reggae rhythm and intoning the words a couple of
hundred times, they stopped and looked at each other. Something, they sensed, had begun to take shape inside them, something that might just serve to revive their flagging spirits. They
didn't know it at the time, but that something was rage.

The two of them were now getting together not just on Saturdays but more or less on a daily basis. Ishihara often spent the
night as well, and Nobue's neighbors had come to regard them
as a devoted homosexual couple. They didn't actually engage
in sexual activity together, but they did frequently embrace for
no particular reason, laughing meaninglessly, and often cooked
their own specialties for each other—mostly things like instant
ramen or plastic packaged retort foods or reheated box lunches.
They would dine facing each other across Nobue's small table,
after which they'd sit side by side hugging their knees and
watching a video of *Rain Man* or *Stand By Me* or *Lethal Weapon*
or some other saga of male bonding. And at night, when anxiety
or fear made sleep impossible for either of them, they would lie
together in one futon, even going so far as to hold hands.

Another month went by. On a night when a cold wind was blowing and drifts of fallen leaves rustled and shivered and swirled in corners of the parking lot, the two of them agreed that they wanted to eat something that would warm even the cockles of their hearts, and with that goal in mind they set out for the convenience store. On the way, Nobue stopped any number of times and pressed his hand to his cheek. Each time he did so, Ishihara would skip around him, chanting in that singsongy way of his, "What's the matter, Nobu-chin? Nobu-chin, what's wrong? Your cheek's all red, are you okay? Tell me, Nobu-chin!"

"It hurts whenever the cold wind hits it," Nobue would reply, and invariably add, "Fucking hell!"

"I love that expression," Ishihara said this time, and launched into a strangely coherent reminiscence.

"You know, Nobu-chin, I was always a good kid, and my father was a good guy too, so we never had any big problems when I was growing up, but when I was in middle school, I don't know how to explain it exactly, but the fact that we never had any problems started to feel like a lot of pressure on me, because I wasn't just like him—we were different—but I didn't know how to get that across to him, and it bothered me a lot, I really worried about it, and I still remember one night, him and me and my mother, we were watching this comedy show on TV—it might've been *The Drifters*—and one of the comedians came out with some stupid gag that wasn't even funny, just some dumb catchphrase like, 'Oops! I'm a ba-a-a-a-ad boy!' or whatever, and my father starts laughing like crazy, and as he's laughing he's tapping me on the head—*tap! tap! tap!*—and I told him not to do that because it hurt, and he's like, 'Oh, don't be such a grouch,' and keeps on tapping, and finally I knocked his hand away and shouted, 'STOP IT!' at the top of my lungs, and my mother's, like, stunned, and my father gets all flustered and goes, 'What got into *you* all of a sudden? You're not going to let a little thing like *this* bother you, are you?' and he raps me on the head again, only harder, trying to make a joke out of it, like we're just playing around, and that's when I felt myself snap. It was a definite physical sensation, and I knew I was just about this close to stabbing him with a kitchen knife or bashing his head in with a metal bat or something, but instead I said, *Fucking hell!* And when I said that, my father exploded. He's like, 'HOW DARE YOU SAY THAT TO ME!' But then, right after shouting at me like that, with the audience on TV still screaming with laughter, he suddenly starts crying like a little girl, just blubbering, and my mother puts her arm around his shoulder, like this, and goes, 'He didn't really mean it, dear!' But the truth is, if it hadn't been for *Fucking hell!* I'm pretty sure I would've killed him. And then, after that, every time I shouted *Fucking hell!* it was like, I don't know, like whatever I was feeling would turn into something I could see with my eyes, oozing right out of me. I mean, not all mushy like puke or something, but . . . I mean, it would suck if it looked like puke, right? Yuck."

There were hardly any other customers in the convenience store, it being a weekday and a slow time of the evening. The two of them made straight for the magazine corner as if drawn by gravitational force and spent the next thirty minutes leafing through periodicals with pictures of naked girls. "Whoa—look at the size of these nipples," Nobue would remark, and Ishihara would say, "This one's got teats like a goat," and start bleating. Nobue pointed at another picture and wondered, "Why does she have this, like, dark red five-o'clock shadow on her crotch?" and

Ishihara said, "Here's one with pimples on her butt, and they're in the shape of the Big Dipper!" They both burst out laughing at that one and bounced up and down twelve or fifteen times, magazines still in hand. Ishihara then approached the register and asked the clerk, a sweet-faced youth of about his own age, "Do you have any food that can warm the cockles of hearts?" The young clerk tilted his head, thinking. "Let me see . . . cockles of hearts, that's a difficult one. May I ask you to wait a moment?" He called for the manager, a serious-looking, bespectacled man of maybe thirty. "The customer is looking for a dish that will warm cockles of hearts," the sweet-faced clerk said, and the manager muttered, "I see," and with his arms crossed and a look of intense concentration began walking up and down the aisles. The clerk marched along behind him, and Ishihara and Nobue followed. Finally the manager selected a package of *nabeyaki udon*, an earthy noodle dish that required only fire and water to prepare. "This ought to do the trick," he said.

Dangling their plastic bags containing the nabeyaki udon and, for dessert, two Ricecake Snow Creams, they next visited the video store, where they rented a tape of the old TV series *Combat!* entitled "Tanks vs. Artillery." On the way back to the apartment, Ishihara stopped at a vending machine and bought a jar of One Cup Sake, which he opened on the spot and proceeded to drink as they resumed walking. A middle-aged drunk was heading toward them from the opposite direction, singing quietly. Whether he'd been in a fight or simply fallen down somewhere, the man was bleeding from a cut on the edge of his lip, his white shirt was muddy, his thinning hair pointed in every direction, and his necktie was stretched out of shape and wrinkled, but as he passed them he was still singing contentedly to himself.

"I know that song," Ishihara said. "What's it called again?"

" 'Dreams Anytime,' " said Nobue.

They were watching Sergeant Saunders take on a German tank single-handedly when Nobue said, "O-Sugi and Yano-rin used to love that song. They always said we'd have to use it for the theme song one of these nights." He began humming "Dreams Anytime," and Ishihara joined in. Soon they were singing at the tops of their voices, and Nobue's eyes were brimming with tears. Ishihara too began choking up. "Who killed them?" he whimpered. "Who killed Kato-kichi and O-Sugi and Yano-rin?"

"Who do you think?" Nobue sobbed. "Those women, of course! Ishi-kun, the truth is, I did some investigating. Remember that list Kato-kichi made for us, with the Oba-sans' names and addresses? I've been staking out the places they live, and I'll tell you, they're on their guard, they're being very careful. They never gather in one place anymore, not even to go sing karaoke together. You know the one whose face we saw, the one who blew chunks when you ripped off her ski mask? Well, you can imagine how I felt, after staking out her apartment all day, when I finally saw her. I knew it was her right away—I could feel it in my cheek! These bitches are scary, man, and I don't just mean their faces. I mean, they've got some serious fuckin' weapons. . . ."

As Nobue was making these points in his new, somewhat nasal voice, a German soldier on the TV screen had been bellowing into a wireless radio. "The enemy is spread out all over the hill!" he bellowed now. "It's impossible to pinpoint a place to strike!"

Nobue and Ishihara turned to look at the TV. A German SS officer in a black form-fitting uniform shouted back into a radio of his own.

"*Dummkopf!* Then just blow up the entire hill!"

They made the journey to an all-night bookstore and bought a map of Greater Tokyo. Back at the apartment, they rewarmed a couple of jars of One Cup Sake. Taking small sips so as not to get drunk too quickly, and snacking on smoked squid, they spread the map out on the floor and focused their attention on Chofu City.

"All right, Ishi-kun, I'll read the names and addresses, and you take these pins and mark the spot where each one lives. Approximately is good enough." Nobue opened the college notebook Kato had left behind and read the relevant information for each of the four Midoris. The first two lived near the center of town, the third on the northern edge, and the fourth on the western outskirts. Ishihara also put a pin at the location of the Flower Petal Women's Junior College dormitory, the abode of the girl with the misaligned eyes and terrifying face. The head of each pin was a little plastic sunflower.

"Pretty wide area," Ishihara muttered. "It'd be cool if I was a giant, and this map was the real Chofu, and I could just step on it, like this, and they'd all be dead. Squash 'em like marshmallows."

Nobue stared at the map between Ishihara's feet as the latter trod in a slow, city-leveling circle. What to do? The Tokarev was long gone—not that it would have done them much good against these four women. They were clearly not just your average Oba-sans. The newspaper had said they'd used a rocket launcher. Where in Japan could you get your hands on a rocket launcher? Nobue had once seen an ex–Green Beret on TV who was a resident of Japan—maybe these women were the wives of geezers like that.

Ishihara was taking a felt pen to the first spot on the map where he'd placed a pin. He drew the *omanko* mark, which consisted of two concentric circles bisected by a long vertical line, with wavy hairs radiating out from the doughnut, and was instantly recognizable to any Japanese middle school boy as a symbol for the female reproductive organ. "Omanko One, Suzuki Midori," he intoned, writing the name. He proceeded to sketch a pair of fat, warped lips, protruding teeth, and a distended tongue upon which he placed a coiled, steaming turd; added a pair of large, deformed nostrils, into each of which he inserted a sharpened number 2 pencil; and finally completed the portrait with bulging eyes and a dialogue balloon inscribed with the words "Oh, yes, YES! Stick in a BIGGER ONE!"

"Ishi-kun," Nobue groaned, "stop messing around and help me figure out what we should do."

Ishihara responded by drawing one big omanko mark that covered the whole of Chofu on the map.

"*Dummkopf!*" he said. "We'll just blow up the entire city."

10

Until We Meet Again

"The entire city of Chofu—we'll blow it away, blow it away, blow it away, blow it away . . ."

Ishihara continued chanting this even after he crawled under the covers, and eventually he got himself so worked up that his moist eyes began to glow with a light of their own, and he couldn't sleep. He needed to do something but didn't know what, and though he himself wondered if this wasn't crossing a line better left uncrossed, he gripped Nobue's hand tightly with one of his own and rubbed his own chest and stomach with the other, moaning, *Ah . . . ahh . . . ahhn!* as he did so. Nobue was understandably startled and disconcerted.

"Ishi-kun! What're you doing? That's not even funny, man. In the first place, to go to sleep holding hands, if you think about it—shit, even if you don't think about it—is pretty fuckin' weird. But, you know, when my cheek was hurting really bad, I used to get so pissed off and frustrated and lonely, and I felt like at that rate I was just going to keep spiraling down, so I went ahead and let you hold my hand when we slept, even though I knew it wasn't normal, but, please, if you're gonna hold my hand, don't be rubbing your body and making those creepy noises, all right?"

"But it feels so *good*," Ishihara murmured, bending his knees and gyrating his hips. "You try it too, Nobu-chin: *Blow it away, blow it away, blow it away*—you keep saying that in your head, and when you touch your body it feels like you're going to come, like you're just going to let go and start squirting—*floop, floop, floop, FLOOOOP!*"

"Ishi-kun, listen to me, that's fucked up, what you're doing." Nobue gently freed his hand and wiped his sweaty palm on the sheets. He wasn't sure if the sweat was his or Ishihara's. "Here's the deal, Ishi-kun. We just realized that we have an important mission to fulfill, right? You know we can't allow the courageous deaths of Yano-rin and Kato-kichi and O-Sugi to be in vain. We can't let them die for nothing!" Sugiyama and Yano and Kato had died prancing on a moonlit beach, dressed in bizarre costumes and singing "Love Me to the Bone," but somehow none of that entered into Nobue's recollection of events. His own words had moved him powerfully, and now tears welled up in his eyes. "We have a mission to fulfill, Ishi-kun, an appointed task. You're the only friend I have left, it's true, but I think it would be a big mistake for us to turn homo. We can't let their deaths be in vain!" he said again, and the emotionally charged words caused him to furrow his brow and make a face like a gorilla sucker-punched with a baseball bat, but a moment later he was sitting bolt upright in bed, his hair standing on end as Ishihara let loose with an earsplitting howl: "HOMO-O-O-O-O-O-O!" Twice more he howled—HOMO-O-O-O-O-O-O! HOMO-O-O-O-O-O-O-O!—then smiled and said, "Awesome!" Nobue was pretty sure that not even God knew what that "awesome" was supposed to mean.

"Ishi-kun, listen to me. A long time ago—or, actually, I guess it was fairly recently—I read this story in a girls' manga called, um, 'Erika's Flower Garden,' about a dancer named Erika who can't find any work, and she gets this boyfriend who's younger than her whose name is Yoshi-bo, and Yoshi-bo's an unemployed dancer too, and they start living together, and a year goes by, two years go by, and then one day they both realize: *This is no good.* They love each other, of course, and they take good care of each other, but if they stay together it's like they're complete, everything's resolved, and they won't keep pursuing their dreams. That's what they realize, and Erika, looking back later on, she tells us in like a voice-over, 'It was a horrifying epiphany.' And so, even though they're in love, they decide to split up. You understand, Ishi-kun? Even though they're in love. And it's the same for you and me. If we became homos, something would come full circle, and the deaths of Yano-rin and the others would end up being for nothing. I mean . . . how to put this? I feel like if we don't do something soon, if we don't take some positive action, we'll lose our fighting spirit, our eye of the tiger, and never get it back."

Ishihara repeated the words "horrifying epiphany" and muttered, *That's some stupid shit.*

"All right, then, Nobu-chin, you tell me: how're we gonna wipe out the rest of those Oba-sans?"

Nobue furrowed his brow again. This time he looked like a hippopotamus who'd accidentally sat in a puddle of hot mustard.

"That's what we have to figure out, Ishi-kun, that's what I'm trying to say. Thinking is our only option now. We've got to think and think and think, until we think it all the way through."

Ishihara said, "How about if we take that junior college girl to their house and make her sing and dance?" and Nobue shook his head and told him to be serious. "Well, then, Nobu-chin, why don't you stop talking all this big talk about Erika and homos and I don't know what and come up with a concrete plan?" He sat up, reached for the map, and spread it out between them on the futon.

"They all live so far apart," Nobue said, his brow still wrinkled. The wrinkles disappeared with Ishihara's next words.

"What about an atomic bomb?"

Two days later, Ishihara and Nobue were in Setagaya—a tony section of Tokyo they'd never set foot in before. At a fruit stand in front of the station they bought a package of gourmet strawberries. "I wonder if he'll really meet with us," Nobue muttered, and Ishihara, skipping in circles around him, chanted, "He will, he will, I know he will!"

The day before, they'd gone to a bookstore and asked the lady at the register if she had any books on how to build an atomic bomb. Her reply had been curt and in the negative, so they'd gone on to a video rental shop. "Are there any films or documentaries that teach you how to build an atomic bomb?" they asked, and the long-haired dude at the register said, "Hell, yes." The movie they rented was entitled *The Man Who Invented Fire*, and it was produced and directed by someone named Haseyama Genjiro. Haseyama Genjiro's house was in Setagaya. Nobue had found the address in the *Japan Association of Film Directors Directory*. A photo of Haseyama Genjiro accompanied his entry, and Nobue and Ishihara both thought he was handsome.

The house was on the outskirts of a section of town noted for being where the richest people lived. Nobue pressed the chime on the intercom at the front gate, and a woman's voice said, "Who's there?"

"We've come to see Haseyama-sensei," Nobue carefully enunciated into the speaker. "We're fans of his work."

"You didn't see him out there?" the voice said. "He just stepped out to buy some cigarettes. He'll be coming back soon."

The two of them had waited in front of the house for twelve or thirteen minutes when Haseyama Genjiro, looking just like his photo, came sprinting around the corner at top speed and skidded to a stop in front of the gate. He had a carton of short Hopes tucked under his arm.

"Shit," he said bitterly, looking down at his watch. "Just can't shave off those last ten seconds!" He bent over for a moment, gasping for breath, then straightened up when he noticed the two visitors. "Who are you?" he said. "What do you want?"

"We're fans," they answered more or less in unison. Nobue held out the package of strawberries and added, "Will you teach us how to make an atomic bomb?"

"Ha," Haseyama Genjiro said. "I get that all the time." He

then took a step back and studied them closely. "But you two have interesting faces. Follow me. We can talk in the park."

He led them to a city park about five hundred meters away. It was a big park with tennis courts, athletic fields, and a small botanical garden. The three of them sat on an embankment overlooking the tennis courts. Haseyama Genjiro was wearing a Nike warm-up suit, Air Jordan II basketball shoes, a cap with the Chicago Bulls logo, and Ray-Ban sunglasses. Nobue and Ishihara gazed at his profile and thought, *How cool can you get?* He was, as far as they could see, the very essence of that quality. A group of four deeply tanned, late-fortyish women were playing an energetic and shrilly vocal game of doubles on one of the courts. Nobue wondered if the members of the terrifying Midori Society were tennis players too.

"How'd you get that scar on your cheek?" Haseyama Genjiro asked Nobue, whose heartbeat quickened as he replied:

"Got knifed."

"In a fight? You don't look the type."

"The thing is," said Ishihara, "we're in a battle to the death with a group of Oba-sans."

"You're WHAT?" Haseyama Genjiro said, raising his voice a bit. "A battle with Oba-sans? And you want to use a nuclear weapon on them?"

"Yes, sir. They live in different parts of Chofu, so there's no way to kill them all without one." Ishihara looked at his own distorted face reflected in the Ray-Bans. Even he had to admit it was some face.

"Oba-sans are a problem for everybody," Haseyama Genjiro

said in an anguished tone. "Oba-sans, to put it in somewhat diffi-cult terms, are life-forms that have stopped evolving. And anyone can turn into an Oba-san. Young women, of course, but even young men, even middle-aged men—even children. You turn into an Oba-san the instant you lose the will to evolve. It's a bloodcur-dling truth that no one seems to recognize. Bloodcurdling!"

"Is it easy to make an atomic bomb?" Nobue asked, and Haseyama Genjiro shook his head sadly.

"It's impossible unless you have plutonium," he said, then clapped them both on the shoulders and said, "But don't give up hope. There's an even better weapon, and it's easy to make. I'll tell you how right now, if you've got ten minutes. You'd better take notes."

Nobue and Ishihara withdrew their entire savings from their accounts at the bank and post office. Unfortunately, their entire savings amounted to only 12,930 yen, so they had no choice but to turn to their parents. Nobue wired his, saying that an emer-gency had arisen and he needed money immediately. Ishihara called home and explained that he'd caught a bad cold that had turned into a life-threatening illness, send cash. His par-ents promptly dispatched a crate of tangerines and a package of vacuum-packed eels, along with a note saying, *We're having a hard time ourselves—hope this helps you pull through!* Eels and tangerines wouldn't be of any use at all in building the weapon as outlined by Haseyama Genjiro. Nobue's parents eventually sent emergency aid to the tune of 300,000 yen, but that wasn't nearly enough.

"It'll cost that much just to rent the helicopter," Ishihara complained, and then got personal, saying, "What is your family, a bunch of paupers?"

"Look who's talking!" Nobue replied with some heat. "All *your* people sent were some fucking eels!"

Having at last discovered a practical and feasible method for blowing up Chofu City, however, they weren't about to get into a serious fight. They spent a few basically enjoyable minutes slapping each other's cheeks and foreheads: Pauper! Eel-boy! Pauper! Eel-boy! But the fact remained that they still didn't have sufficient funds to build the weapon. Their own parents having proved so unreliable, they now realized they had no choice but to contact the parents of Sugioka and Yano and Kato and Sugiyama. It took several drafts to get the letter right.

"Once, there was a Group of Six Good Friends. They helped and encouraged one another, drank together sometimes, and sang together, celebrating their youth, standing shoulder to shoulder as they struggled to survive in the concrete desert of the big city. However!! The unthinkable happened. Fate decreed that four of these innocent young men were to be taken from us, snatched from this world—nay, snatched from the Group of Six!—before their rightful time. It is our hope to commemorate these precious lives with a collection of pure, heartfelt, and poignant recollections gathered from those who knew and remember our departed pals best. Long live the Group of Six Good

Friends! We are hoping that you who share our sorrow will support the publication of this effort by contributing five hundred thousand yen. . . ."

A total of one-point-seven million yen came in. That they came up three hundred thousand short of their goal was because Sugiyama's parents sent only two hundred thousand, his mother appending an apologetic note to the effect that at the moment her husband was out of work and they were barely able to make ends meet. But Nobue and Ishihara pressed their hands together and bowed with gratitude in the direction of Fukushima Prefecture, where Sugiyama's parents lived. In the midst of their own struggles they had sent what they could and would now probably have to live on millet and barnyard grass for a month or two. Ishihara and Nobue were determined not to let that sacrifice be in vain. Failure, they both thought, was simply not an option.

The preparations began.

They leased a small warehouse near Harumi on a two-week renewable contract. Building the weapon in Nobue's apartment was out of the question because of the danger of premature explosion. This was clearly stated in the notes Haseyama Genjiro had dictated to them, which he'd entitled "For a Better Tomorrow."

"For a Better Tomorrow #1: The site of construction should be as spacious and as far from human habitations as possible. . . ."

On the floor of the warehouse, they reassembled a salvaged prefab shed, sealing the interior walls with four layers of reinforced plastic, then took a vow to abstain from any activities that might interfere with their concentration, including drinking, smoking, playing computer games, and masturbating. They then began gathering the materials listed in their notes.

"For a Better Tomorrow #2: Assemble the following items: porcelain plates, alcohol burners, hydroextractor, flasks, drip funnel, reflux condenser, separating funnel, glass test tubes (various sizes), thiophosphoric acid syrup, calcium chloride, activated alumina, ethyl alcohol, isopropyl alcohol . . ."

Neither Nobue nor Ishihara had any talent for or experience with this sort of thing, but they found it surprisingly easy to acquire the necessary items at stores that specialized in chemicals and science equipment. Once they had everything, they set to work in all earnestness, poring over Haseyama Genjiro's notes literally hundreds of times as they manipulated the ingredients. Incredibly, not once during the days that followed did they joke or goof around or laugh meaninglessly or tease or ridicule each other. What's more, they restricted themselves to simple meals of sandwiches and coffee and never ate to the point of satiation. They mastered the operation of the reflux condenser and the separating funnel, and used almost excessive care at every step—whether heating test tubes to precisely three hundred degrees or icing gas-wash bottles for exactly forty-five minutes. Neither of them had ever before had anything to which to dedicate themselves so thoroughly, and they absorbed the basics of chemistry the way sand dunes absorb rain, working relentlessly and rarely catching more than an hour or two of sleep at a time. Gradually they began to feel that they finally understood what it was they'd been so starved for all their lives, what it was they really wanted. It was the first time that either of them had ever been able to throw himself into an endeavor so wholeheartedly that nothing else in the world mattered or rated as a distraction. They not only refrained from masturbation, for example—they forgot even to think about it.

"For a Better Tomorrow #3: Convert the ethylene and propylene to ethylene oxide and propylene oxide, respectively. CAUTION: Both oxides are highly flammable when mixed with air. Take special care not to expose these substances to any potential source of ignition, such as open flames, excessive heat, sparks, etc. Use well-iced gas-wash bottles. . . ."

Haseyama Genjiro's notes were precise down to the smallest detail—and therefore exceedingly dangerous in the wrong hands. But perhaps he had judged from looking at his two protégés' faces that they would never succeed in constructing the item in question. He had asked them to come back and show him when they'd produced one-five-hundredth of the necessary material, thinking that if they succeeded in making even that much, he might reference their work in his next film. But by the time they began accumulating ethylene oxide and propylene oxide, Ishihara and Nobue had forgotten all about Haseyama Genjiro.

"For a Better Tomorrow #4: Combine the ethylene oxide and propylene oxide, in the ratio indicated above, in an appropriate vessel. A tank of some sort works best. . . .

"For a Better Tomorrow #5: The fuse is of utmost importance. It must be what is commonly referred to as a delayed fuse, to trigger the explosion some seconds (see chart below) after the tank bursts upon impact with the ground. . . ."

Various types of vessels were suggested in the notes, from plastic gas cans to milk bottles, but Ishihara and Nobue finally decided on a container of their own invention. They got hold of a very large and sturdily constructed tripod case of the sort used by film production companies and devised a thick, insulated vinyl bag to fit inside it. They filled the plastic bag with their mixture, fitted it into the tripod case—leaving not a centimeter of wiggle room—and covered it with a false bottom. On top of this they gently placed a much smaller tripod than the case was designed for. They made the delayed fuse, which would work on the same general principle as a hand grenade, out of one of those cylindrical tins that hold two hundred nonfiltered Peace cigarettes. They wrapped black gunpowder from dissected firecrackers inside a tight roll of thick paper, which they packed inside the tin, along with a number of thin leaden tubes from toy model kits, also filled with gunpowder. They set a spring-loaded striker in such a way that it would release on impact, igniting the delay powder in the little leaden tubes, which in turn would ignite the fuse. Finally, they surrounded the fuse with triggering explosive and blasting powder. One Peace tin was all they needed. Nineteen days after they'd begun their work, the weapon was complete.

It was a fuel-air explosive (FAE), also called a thermobaric bomb, but more commonly known as the poor man's nuclear weapon.

On a sunny winter's day, Nobue and Ishihara arrived at the offices of a helicopter charter service at Haneda Airport. They were carrying a Betacam video camera they'd rented and two tripod cases. They'd already made a reservation, and the transaction

was processed quickly and uneventfully. Ishihara was posing as
a cameraman employed by a German TV station, and Nobue as
his assistant. No one would ever imagine homegrown terrorists
chartering a heli for two hours at a hundred fifty thousand yen
an hour. Besides, they hadn't requested a flight over the Imperial
Palace or the Diet building but rather the bland Tokyo suburb of
Chofu City. Sitting on a plush sofa in the waiting room sipping
cups of roasted-rice tea supplied by a young lady in black stockings, they wrote random names and addresses on the paperwork,
scribbled on the dotted lines, paid cash in advance, and got a
receipt.

"All set?" said the young pilot when they were introduced at
the helipad. Nobue and Ishihara took one look at him and nearly
squealed like teenage girls: he was a dead ringer for the late Sugioka. "We've removed the rear door to facilitate filming."

Parked in the center of a big yellow-painted circle was a vintage Sikorsky. The Sugioka-look-alike pilot helped them climb
into the rear seat with their video camera and tripod cases.
Nobue held the camera in his lap. "Here we go," said the pilot
as the rotors began spinning and they lifted off. Below them, on
the ground, the clerk who'd just accepted their three hundred
thousand yen was smiling and waving moronically.

"We'll head straight for Chofu, then, is that correct?" the
pilot said over the intercom. Ishihara, who was already having
the time of his life, replied in a queer falsetto voice, "That's correct, dahhhling!" The pilot turned to give him a brief stare but
then decided to let it go—no doubt there were a lot of eccen-
tric people in TV and film. "Which part of Chofu?" he asked.
"Chofu Station, please," said Nobue, and both he and Ishihara,

buffeted by the wind coming through the open door, burst into uncontrollable laughter. The pilot spoke again.

"We'll arrive in fifteen minutes."

Henmi Midori was at home watching *Emmanuelle 4*. The film had been broadcast on WOWOW a couple of nights before, and she'd recorded it to video. It was early afternoon. A while ago she had called Tomiyama Midori, only to hear that Tomii was busy visiting with her son and didn't have time to talk. She had then leafed absently through the textbook for an English conversation class she'd recently begun attending. Her body felt fuzzy and itchy inside, however, reminding her that it was about time for her period to begin, and the English letters began to look like microscopic photos of sperm, so she'd closed the book and inserted the tape of the sophisticated soft-porn film she'd set her VCR to record in the wee hours of the night before last. The original Emmanuelle, a middle-aged woman now, played a part in this film as well. How many years had it been since she'd watched the first film in the series with the man she'd been dating at the time? The man had told her that she bore a certain resemblance to Sylvia Kristel, and that night they'd slept together for the first time. It was perfectly clear to Henmi Midori that Sylvia Kristel, even in this later film and with a sagging middle-aged derriere, didn't look like her in the least. Had the man just been feeding her a line, or was it that he liked her so much that he really imagined a resemblance? As she watched the film and thought back to those times, the itchy sensation worked its way deeper into her body. She was thinking that if she comforted herself now, in the middle of the day, she'd probably end up feeling pretty pathetic, when she noticed a sort of gasoline smell. A split-second later, Henmi Midori knew no more. In the space of an instant, she was burned to a fine ash, along with her entire house.

Tomiyama Midori was enjoying something she'd lost for some time but had regained after the battle on the seashore above Atami—conversation with her son. Osamu had become a regular chatterbox. He talked about school, his favorite TV shows, his friends, girls in his class, and especially American pro basketball, with which he was utterly obsessed. He watched all the games on TV and recorded them to review again and again, and he spoke endlessly of his favorite players and how "off the hook" their skills were. His animated face and shining eyes were adorable and radiated an energy that seemed to seep into and illuminate Tomiyama Midori's own being. She had received a phone call from Henmi Midori earlier but had cut it short, unwilling to sacrifice even a minute of this precious time with her son. Hemii would only have wanted to reminisce about Atami or talk about the tall young sales rep at her office. "There's a T-shirt I've just got to have," Osamu was saying, and Tomiyama Midori immediately made up her mind that she would find it for him at any cost. Apparently it was a T-shirt with a picture of someone named Charles Barkley dunking a basketball over Godzilla's head. "If Barkley and Godzilla ever really did get into a fight," Osamu said, "Barkley would win for sure, that's how awesome he is!" Before leaving her condo, Tomiyama Midori had helped her son into his hooded, child-sized Burberry slicker and wrapped herself in a mink half-coat she was paying for in thirty-six installments. They were now walking hand in hand down a poplar-lined street beneath the clear and pale blue winter sky. Such a tiny hand, and yet it contained all the necessary cells and nerves and pulsing blood vessels, she was thinking, and feeling such a surge of love that tears welled up in her eyes, when Osamu pointed at the sky and said, "Look! A chopper!" Neither of them noticed the black cylinder descending from it. They had taken a few more rustling steps through the fallen poplar leaves that covered the street, when the tripod case, after a drop of a thousand meters, hit the ground at a bus stop outside the north entrance to Chofu Station. It burst apart, as did the vinyl bag inside, releasing a gaseous mixture of ethylene oxide and propylene oxide, which instantly dissipated into the air over the entire city of Chofu. A few seconds later, the Peace tin exploded. This set off, not the sort of blast that expands outward, but an instantaneous combustion of the atmosphere itself. Tomiyama Midori and her son, along with all the other people crowding the streets in the center of town, simply evaporated in fire.

Because Suzuki Midori was airing her futon on the veranda of her apartment on the outskirts of town, where the combustion didn't quite reach, she experienced a somewhat grizzlier death. She had recently begun listening to Mozart, and that afternoon she'd gone to the CD section of a department store and bought Piano Concertos Nos. 22 and 23. She listened to them as she made and ate a spaghetti lunch at her apartment, and then, inspired by the clear blue winter sky, decided to air her futon. Each note emanating from Vladimir Ashkenazy's piano was like a tangible, sparkling jewel, and the music seemed to seep into her very bones. She wondered how it was that she'd come to feel Mozart so deeply, but the answer occurred to her almost at once. It all had to do with that night at the Atami seashore. A certain sense of superiority she felt at possessing such a powerful secret, a secret such as no one else possessed or could even imagine, was the thread that tied her to Mozart's sensuality. Unless you had a legitimate sense of entitlement you couldn't really understand the beauty of Mozart, she was thinking as she carried the futon out to the railing, intoxicated with the adagio of the second movement, and detected a strange odor. The next instant, fire filled her entire field of vision. The explosion itself didn't reach her veranda, but because it devoured all the oxygen in the vicinity in zero-point-one seconds, she found herself clawing at her own breast as her face twisted into a hideous mask. The Mozart was drowned out by the all-consuming roar of her own throat collapsing, and with blood dripping from her broken nails and the gouges she'd dug into her own chest, she collapsed and expired there on the veranda, sandwiched in her own futon.

The junior college girl with the misaligned eyes was attending a lecture on child psychology in the big lecture hall at her school and wondering why no one in the crowded room took any of the seats around her. It made her sad to think it might be because her face was so scary, as her brother had always told her when she was little and as the manager at MOS Burger had said just recently when she went to apply for a part-time job. In her loneliness, she decided to try and summon up one of her ghost friends to talk to. Sugioka's ghost was always the first to appear, and today was no exception. But as he emerged from the mists, it was clear that he wasn't the same sorrowful and docile spirit as always. He was smirking. "You're all gonna die," he told her. *What are you talking about? Quit being so weird, or I won't show you my boobies anymore,* she was about to reply, when the lecture hall disintegrated. "Take *that!*" Sugioka's ghost snickered. The junior college girl knew right away that she had passed over. She experienced an odd mixture of sorrow and relief on finding that her entire face was gone.

Takeuchi Midori was in her car in the parking structure beneath the Ito Yokado superstore, and she, along with three other housewives who happened to be in their cars, survived both the fuel-air explosion and the depletion of oxygen in the immediate atmosphere. At first she thought it was either an earthquake or a nuclear war, and she sat in her car with all the windows rolled up for a full five minutes, then got out and climbed over the mounds of collapsed bricks and out into the street, where an astonishing sight awaited her. The town was in ruins. Burning automobiles sent up whirling billows of smoke, and charred bodies lay scattered over the ground as far as the eye could see.

Nobue and Ishihara were so taken aback by the magnitude of the explosion that they briefly stopped laughing, but the Sugioka-look-alike pilot, who barely managed to steady the helicopter after it was rocked by the blast, wet his pants in panic and outrage. His lips turned bone-white, and his thoughts were all mashed up—*Who are these two guys? What just happened? What'll they say when I get back to the office? To think I put up with that asshole sergeant in the SDF just so I could get a chopper license!*—and he began to weep. When Nobue said, "Drop us somewhere in the mountains, where no one's around," he nodded and said, "*Hai,*" in a pathetic voice before veering off at full speed toward Chichibu.

He set the helicopter down at a rest area on a snowy, deserted road in the Chichibu Mountains. Nobue and Ishihara said, "See ya!" and started walking away, but the pilot called out, "Wait a minute!" and came running after them. "I can't go back to my office! I mean, I'm pretty sure it'd mean the death penalty, right?"

The three of them stood side by side pissing in the restroom trough, and then drank cans of steaming hot coffee, fresh from the vending machine.

"Don't worry," Nobue said. "Something that big, it'll take 'em at least a week before they get around to trying to figure out who did it. There's no motive, and the address I wrote down at your office puts me in Niigata, so they'll probably figure it was done by right-wing Russians or something. Kinda chilly up here," he added, and took the lead in marching down the mountain.

"Who are you guys?" the pilot asked with a mixture of fear and respect playing in his features as he followed them down.

"Nobody knows," said Ishihara. "We've been ignored all our lives, so nobody knows who we are."

Nobue wondered if the woman with the unbelievable body in the apartment across the way had died, and decided she probably had. *I wish ones like that, at least, could have lived*, he thought, and felt, just for a moment, a twinge of guilt.

Ishihara began humming "Until We Meet Again." He could feel his entire body sizzling with energy as he did so. Nobue joined in, but the pilot was apparently too young to remember the song. *We'll have to teach it to him*, Ishihara thought. *Four of us may have died, but now we're already finding new blood, and there are any number of replacements out there. In two or three months maybe we'll even be able to hold another Karaoke Blast.*

He felt really good and started laughing that familiar laugh of his.